Patrons of the Dark Arts

Jeffrey Thomas

Publication Credits

The Promotion at Newcastle appeared on the Patreon website Jeffrey Thomas is Creating Weird Fiction on 1-11-15

The Doom That Came to Hamletville appeared on JTICWF 1-16-15

Southern Cross appeared on JTICWF 1-24-15

Blue Mannequins appeared on JTICWF 2-8-15

The Convergence appeared on JTICWF 2-15-15

Cracked Lips appeared on JTICWF 2-24-15

Always appeared on JTICWF 3-10-15

Carny Goddess was first published as part of the novella *Beyond the Door*, Delirium Books, 2011. Originally conceived as a standalone piece, it appeared in this form on JTICWF 5-2-15

Waltered States was first published as a portion of the story *Nocturnal Emissions* in the collection of the same name, Dark Regions Press, 2012. I later tweaked it slightly to work as a standalone piece, and it appeared in this form on JTICWF 5-1-17

The Afterlife of Jacob B. Coppins is original to this collection.

DEDICATION

To my readers, who sustain me.

CONTENTS

ACKNOWLEDGMENTS

With much gratitude to all my supporters at Patreon, whatever their pledge level. As of the date of publication, those who initially pledged $10-$20 a month are:

Patrick Shawn Bagley
Josh Boone
Jason Carella
Matthew Carpenter
Susan Carr Sears
Pamela Chillemi-Yeager
Donald Cobb
Lou Columbus
Sam Cowan
Nikki Guerlain
Tim Feely
Christopher Hendryx
Nicolas Huck
Lee Dong-Hyun
Michael Sean LeSueur
Kevin Lightburn
Tom Lynch
Krista McCrea
Minh Nguyen
Carl Noble
Paul Ramage
Joseph Rodgers
Michael Sauers
Daniel Schenkel
Jonathan K. Stephens
Danyal Bayer Vierheller
Wendy Thomas Walsh
Thomas Weiss
And with special thanks, once more, to Walter Egan for the generous use of his lyrics and persona.

THE PROMOTION AT NEWCASTLE

The little office in the northwest corner of the seventeenth floor had been disused ever since the downsizing that had hollowed out the building as a plague would decimate a village. Though there had been numerous available offices in Boorman's department from which he might have chosen, he hadn't been given the chance. Boorman's manager had assigned this one to him. Anyway, it was no worse than the others as far as he could tell, and he was grateful for having been given this new position, just as he was grateful that he had been spared during the mass layoff at Newcastle last year. As tiny as this office was – barely enough to accommodate a steel desk that seemed too large to have fit through the door, and a single filing cabinet – at least he had moved from the honeycomb of cubicles he had been fixed in for the first four years of his employment.

No, he wasn't going to complain about one thing, lest he be called upstairs to the nineteenth floor to the manager's office. He recalled that apocalyptic day when, one by one, his manager had summoned up to his office every one of the workers who was to be laid off from

1

Newcastle. Boorman had kept his head low over his keyboard, his heart clattering like its keys, waiting to be called...but by the end of the day, he hadn't been.

He remembered, too, right after the downsizing, his coworker Lina raging that she was going to go up there and give him a piece of her mind. "I'm doing the work of three people now, for the pay of one! Not *even* enough pay for one!"

Boorman hadn't seen Lina again after that, which he had regretted, because she was an attractive woman with long, silky blond hair, and furtively watching her had enlivened his work hours somewhat. With her termination he had been left to do the work of four people.

So no, he had never complained about anything , and he felt that in part was why he still worked at Newcastle. And he had finally won some recognition at last, for focusing quietly and obediently on his work! He wasn't about to let it go to his head and start grousing now. Not even when he found a layer of dust as thick as a blotter atop his desk. Not even when he discovered a dead mouse under his chair, so desiccated it was almost turned to a dust ball.

It was with something like drunken euphoria that he shut the door to his office – *HIS OFFICE!* – and caused all the clattering from the warren of cubicles outside to become muffled and distant.

The blinds in his one window had probably been shut for the whole of the past year, since the layoffs. The overhead fluorescents seemed to impart an unhealthy tinge to everything more so than they provided actual light, so he decided to raise the blinds and see if there was a way to crack the window open, so as to let in both sunlight and fresh air, and thereby alleviate some of the room's staleness and dustiness.

He pulled the cord to raise the blinds, and found himself looking out upon a ledge. The ledge entirely ringed this level of the building, its uppermost levels being tiered like a wedding cake so as to make the office tower gradually taper. The ledge, with its slightly raised edge, was covered with fine gravel. Sprawled upon this bed of gravel were three human corpses.

Two were men, in tattered gray business suits. The third was a woman, in a gray jacket and matching skirt. Her body lay partly across the body of one of the men. This man lay face down, but the woman and other man lay on their backs. The limbs of all three were flung out at odd angles or unnaturally bent. All three of them were in an advanced state of decay, all but skeletonized. Their hair had turned wispy and colorless, the woman's long hair stirring dreamily in the breeze like cobwebs.

Boorman stared through the glass without blinking, his face very still, for as long as five minutes. Finally, he loosened his hold on the cord, and let the blinds lower again.

***

On the Friday of his first week in his new office, Boorman's coworker Clausen knocked once on its closed door and let himself in before Boorman could invite him. Clausen's cubicle was on the other side of the one Boorman had vacated. His former neighbor's boozy face was redder than usual, and with his hand still on the knob of the open door, he said, "Well, Boorman, what did you do to climb this rung of the ladder? Did you shine the boss's shoes? Shine his ass with your kisses?"

"I never talk with him," Boorman said, maintaining his mild demeanor. "I just do my job."

"Oh? And I haven't been doing my job, too — for two years longer than you have?"

"Gentleman," said a voice behind Clausen.

Only when Clausen let go of the doorknob and shifted his blocky body to turn did Boorman realize that their manager stood just outside the threshold.

"Oh — hi, sir!" Clausen stammered, somehow turned an even more vivid red.

Their manager was tall and impeccably dressed in a tailored gray suit, wearing a pleasant little smile like an accessory. "Is this new space working out for you, Mr. Boorman?" he asked.

Thin slats of sunlight from the closed blinds behind him striped Boorman's computer screen, an annoyance, and striped the backs of his hands, but he only smiled faintly himself and replied, "Yes, sir."

"Excellent." Their manager started to turn away, but stopped himself and said, "Oh, Mr. Clausen, when you have a free moment could you come up to see me in my office?"

"In your...your office?" Clausen said.

"Yes. I'm sorry – you've probably never been there before. It's on the nineteenth floor." Their manager pointed toward the ceiling.

"Yes, sir…I know where it is," Clausen said. His voice was all but choked to a whisper.

Their manager walked away, and without looking back at Boorman, Clausen left the tiny office in his wake. He shuffled like a man with his ankles in leg irons.

About an hour before it was time to punch out for the weekend, as Boorman was hunched over his keyboard, he heard a heavy thud that sounded like it came from directly behind his chair. He knew, though, that it was on the other side of the window. He flinched, yet resisted the urge to turn around and raise the blinds.

A feeble moan rose up behind him. If words were being uttered – and they did sound like pleas – the glass muffled them to incoherence. Still, Boorman did not swivel around in his chair.

At last, just as he was shutting down his computer and tidying up his desk, the moans – which had been growing fainter and fainter – finally ceased altogether.

Boorman got up from his desk to deposit a few folders into his file cabinet. Only then did he allow his gaze to shift surreptitiously to the window.

Through a thin gap between two of the slats of the blinds, he saw several red spots, sparkling as they caught the late afternoon light, like a child's tiny plastic gems that had been glued to the outside of the glass.

***

The following week, Boorman came in for four hours of overtime on Saturday morning, to catch up on some of the additional work he had inherited with the latest dismissal. As he passed through the open office area with a paper cup of coffee in one hand and a bag of doughnuts in the other, he was struck by the emptiness of all the rows of cubicles.

Poking his head into his office warily, he found it to be gloomier than ever, but then he knew it was raining outside. Slowly he entered, removed his damp suit jacket and draped it over the back of his chair.

He set about his work, moving his computer's mouse with his right hand while he lifted a doughnut with his left. It had frosting as pink as plastic, sprinkled with tiny red candy hearts. The hearts dropped onto his lap and several fell between the keys of his keyboard.

A single knock on his door caused him to jolt in his chair as if someone had fired a gun by his ear. Aside from the security guard at the front desk, he hadn't seen a soul on his way from the lobby to his office door. Before he could find his voice, his door opened and his manager was there, impeccable even on a Saturday, smiling pleasantly.

"I saw you on your way up, Mr. Boorman. Thanks for coming in today. Everything's well?"

"Yes, sir," Boorman managed to get out.

"Excellent." The manager's gaze drifted from Boorman's face to the doughnut poised in his hand. Red candy hearts were scattered about on the desk like something a child had spilled: sequins or faux jewels. The manager frowned as subtly as he smiled. "Mr. Boorman, I

6

believe you know that I disapprove of my people eating in their offices and cubicles."

Boorman made no excuses about it being his breakfast, or this being Saturday. "Yes, sir, I'm sorry. It won't happen again." He dropped the half eaten doughnut back into its paper bag.

His manager's smile returned, and he drew back through the threshold. "Good man," he said.

When his manager shut the door behind him, Boorman's paralyzed heart returned to its duties.

For the rest of that morning, he expected to receive a call, asking him to report upstairs to the nineteenth floor of the Newcastle business tower, but the call didn't come.

Before leaving work at noon, Boorman turned his keyboard upside-down, shook out the tiny red candy hearts, swept them into his hand, and dropped them into his wastebasket.

THE DOOM THAT CAME TO HAMLETVILLE

At the end of every road that led out of Hamletville was somewhere else, somewhere that wasn't Hamletville. It was the hub of the world, the bull's-eye of the target, the very nucleus of culture and business, art and industry. Hamletville was what lay at the vanishing point.

No one outside or even within Hamletville could truly explain why such a nondescript town had developed so rapidly – in just a few generations – into the greatest city in the world. It had grown titanic despite being located in the dead center of the country, far from any ocean port, in a dismally flat expanse...or perhaps it was *because* of being situated there on that open table, free of obstructions. It was suggested the town had originally, either through accident or intuition, been built on some mysterious nodal point of telluric power.

Hamletville thrived, and around the globe countless other cities thrived because of Hamletville, the pulsing heart of the world.

And then one morning just at dawn, the great metropolis of Hamletville went silent and still. Radio and TV broadcasts ceased abruptly. Its myriad lights, dazzling even from afar, were extinguished all at once. The first thought was a power failure, though this had never occurred before, because Hamletville boasted a unique antimatter reactor that derived this antimatter from the planet's Van Allen belt of radiation, and corralled it in a magnetic field. The energy released as matter and antimatter particles annihilated each other powered the entire city and its suburbs.

But it would soon be learned that this was not merely an electrical blackout.

Without communication from its airport, planes could not land in Hamletville, nor did the planes scheduled to depart from its airport do so. That morning, cars bringing commuters in to their jobs, and trucks bringing in freight to feed the ravenous machine that was the city, found all the many roads that flowed into Hamletville thoroughly jammed with unmoving and abandoned vehicles. Those who, out of curiosity and concern, left their own vehicles to venture into the city on foot discovered its innermost streets just as abandoned as the cars blocking the highways. It appeared as if the city had been deserted overnight. Yet, where had its forty million citizens departed to?

The military mobilized to prevent more of the curious or concerned from venturing into Hamletville, and organized a special team to send in for their own investigation. An act of terrorism was feared, but what type of bomb could be detonated that would vaporize every citizen, yet leave not even a scratch in the way of property damage? Even a neutron bomb would leave the bodies of those killed by radiation poisoning, and would still have brought about much destruction. Surely, terrorists hadn't taken all those millions hostage.

This team of military operatives, and several scientists and engineers, was headed by a man named Captain Joseph Rodgers. He had two primary objectives. One, check on the mayor's status. Two, check the status of the power plant, to ensure its present situation, whatever that might be, posed no threat.

Half-crouching and moving forward in furtive, darting spurts, dressed in black and lumpy with gear, signing hand signals to each other, the military men looked like a band of strange performance artists in search of an audience. They soon confirmed with their own eyes what the civilians who'd gone in first reported, and what satellite imagery indicated: that the buildings, the cars in the streets, were intact and stood as if merely waiting to be reoccupied and reanimated by people who had seemingly only been momentarily called away.

At the mayor's home and at City Hall they found no sign of him or any of his family or staff. Rodgers called in their ride to convey them to their next destination in this vast city. Though Hamletville's electricity had gone out, there was no disruptive force at work that prevented a helicopter from flying in and shuttling the operatives.

In fact, they had ascertained that the cars filling the streets were still operational – keys in their ignitions, cold cups of morning coffee still in their cup holders – simply forsaken. Yes, many were damaged in a relatively superficial manner, but this was apparently because their drivers had jumped out of them (in sudden fear?) or been snatched from them while the vehicles were still in movement, these vehicles then having spent their forward momentum by crashing into each other, parking meters, or the fronts of buildings. In the thickly congested streets, where traffic could never attain high speeds, few of the vehicles had been going fast enough to become totaled once they were driverless.

The helicopter set the team down within the fenced off and formerly heavily guarded grounds of the power plant.

No emergency generators had kicked in to supply the antimatter plant, but Rodgers and his crew had copies of keys, tools, flashlights and night vision goggles, and blueprints of the interior right down to the ventilation shafts, accessible via their handheld PCs. Thus prepared, they gained entrance and moved deeper into the power plant.

Rodgers was uneasy any time they passed the glass walls of inner offices, or shining metal surfaces, and did his best to avoid looking directly at them. They had found out, right away, by looking into the windows of the deserted cars outside, that the civilian reports were true: in Hamletville, they could not see their reflections in glass or metal, unless it was an object containing glass or metal that they had brought in with them. One of his soldiers had joked grimly that they had all turned to vampires.

Now, with no sign of lurking terrorists, it was the engineers who led the team to the reactor at the heart of the plant. At no point along the way – through the network of corridors, in offices, in great rooms of silently hulking machinery – did they find so much as a lighted gauge, computer screen, or EXIT sign. The situation was no different in the main control room, nor in the chamber beyond, in which antimatter would be held secure in a magnetic field. They could see that chamber through a wraparound glass window that did not reflect their figures. Nor did their flashlight beams glare back at them; they simply pierced on through.

If there was no electricity, then the magnetic field would be down, but by the same token the process by which new antimatter was teased down from the Van Allen belt into the plant had also ceased operation. Hopefully, whatever antimatter had most recently been extracted and stored had already been spent, cancelled out by its counterpart matter particles. There was no sign of any physical damage from a leak of antimatter, though Rodgers couldn't quite imagine what that would look like, anyway. If the scientists could envision it, they were not sharing the scenario, but they did appear relieved.

Equipment they'd brought informed them that radiation levels were normal. It was deemed safe to venture down into the containment chamber, so they did.

Here, at the center of this room at the center of this plant at the center of the city that was the center of the world, stood a vault. The vault, the size of a shed, had thick lead walls, but more importantly – at least, up until the power failure – the vault had contained the magnetic field that contained harvested antiparticles. There was a thick lead-lined hatch by which technicians could enter the vault. In this hatch at face level was a sliding panel, which when drawn aside revealed a thick glass window. Rodgers himself stepped forward to slide it open, so the technicians could have a peek inside.

The first technician to lean in for a look gazed for a single moment with a slack and befuddled expression, the others watching him expectantly. Then, he cried out inarticulately and abruptly flinched back, bumping violently into the man behind him. One of the scientists quickly took his place, and an instant later jolted back also, babbling in surprise or alarm. Asserting his command, Rodgers shoved his way past the others who crowded in for a peek, to have a look himself, utilizing both his night vision goggles and pointing his flashlight beam through the glass.

The window did not reveal the interior of the vault, but rather looked upon a flat expanse of land under a starless night sky, an open table free of obstructions. This great plain was filled with people – men, women, and children of every age and race – standing naked, upright and unmoving, shoulder-to-shoulder, all of them facing Rodgers with open, slowly blinking eyes and expressionless faces. His flashlight beam could only play across the closest of the figures, who were right on the other side of the metal hatch, but his goggles showed him that this sea of tightly massed bodies reached to the limits of sight. Reached to the vanishing point. Surely, forty million human beings stood on the other side of that window, gazing back at him.

Rodgers recognized the faces of the people closest to the hatch. They were his soldiers, and the scientists and engineers he'd brought in, duplicated. And there, staring directly back at him, was his own doppelganger as well. Identical, but naked, and looking green and luminous due to his night vision goggles. Because of this device, his double's eyes had the appearance of a negative image, with dark sclera and brightly glowing pupils, like the eyes of a cat in the dark.

His doppelganger smiled at him, showing teeth that appeared black in his green-glowing face. It was not so much a smile, though, as an expression of dark hunger. Finally Rodgers, too, recoiled from the window with a racing heart and racing mind.

The rest of the men stole peeks through the window, but none of them could stand looking for long. Those who had peered through entered into highly agitated discussion and debate with each other, in an effort to comprehend what they were experiencing. The last of the team to get a peek was the youngest of Rodgers's soldiers. Perhaps because he was a man filled with youthful bravado, or because he'd been prepared for the sight from having heard the others discussing what they'd seen, he didn't jump back in terror. He stared fixedly through the window at the plain filled with millions of nude, unmoving green figures with brightly glowing eyes.

As Rodgers listened to the scientists throwing theories back and forth, and fumbling these theories to the ground like dropped balls, he glanced at the window again over the shoulder of his young soldier. He saw the soldier's double on the other side of the glass. The soldier's double had taken several steps forward, and was reaching out his hand to the window. Now laying his palm flat against it.

Rodgers's soldier on this side, staring as if in a trance, lifted his own arm to mirror the action.

Rodgers shouted at the man to stop, and lunged toward him to knock him away from the window. It was an intuition he had. But he was a fraction of a second too late, as the two figures pressed their palms together against the glass.

And then, just like that – and unfortunately for the rest of the world, for which this city was its nexus point – Hamletville was occupied again.

SOUTHERN CROSS

Lew Columbus considered it a harmless game, beginning as a diversion on the occasional empty Saturday and later becoming more frequent; maybe several times during the week as well, after he'd got out of work. It had started with an impulse, one Saturday afternoon when he was at the Southern Cross Mall to buy himself a new belt, and refresh his supply of socks and boxers as long as he was there. Before getting around to business, he had idly gone into a CD and comics store to browse their used DVD selection, when he noticed a young woman doing the same. He entered the aisle, stopped not too far from her but not too close, and cocked his head to the side as if to read spines but with his eyes cocked surreptitiously toward her. She was of the type he found most aesthetically appealing; of the type the average American male found appealing; a type that was as common as cute babies but that somehow seemed as elusive as a pot of gold at rainbow's end. A young, long-haired blond in her early twenties, with a curvy figure. She was oblivious to him. He was a man in his forties, nondescript to the point of being as unrecognized as the floor she was standing on. He figured if she were interviewed outside the store and asked if she had been standing on carpet or a hard surface while looking at the DVDs, she wouldn't have been able to answer with sureness. He figured she would be just as much at a loss if asked to describe the man who had been standing in the aisle beside her.

Lew had trailed her into another aisle, where she flipped through CDs, giving her a little more space so as to remain inconspicuous. He continued to steal looks at her. Another man, he knew, would have said something to her like, "Oh, that's a good CD...I have that." Or, "If you like blah-blah, have you ever listened to blah-blah?" But he wasn't that man. She ended up buying a CD, some new artist he wasn't familiar with, and he didn't buy anything lest he lose track of her as she left the store, for his impulse was to continue watching her, admiring her. He followed her out into the mall, walked a discreet distance behind her, appreciating the shifting of her shapely bottom in the apple skin of her blue jeans. When she went down the escalator to the first floor, he descended too. But ultimately, she had slipped into a women's apparel store. He lingered outside a little while, and envisioned her looking at skimpy panties, lacy bras, but finally he had felt too awkward, feared that passersby would notice something off about him, would too plainly read the desire in his tension, the loneliness in his eyes. He had then turned away, and gone on to buy his belt and other items.

It was usually similar young women Lew followed, either natural or dyed blonds, though sometimes they were in their thirties, sometimes teenagers. In the early days he would switch from one to another, as he lost track of one or when a more attractive specimen showed herself, but later on the game became how long he could continue to follow one person throughout the vastness of the Southern Cross Mall. He would sit a table or two away in the food court, or boldly stand right behind her in line for a coffee, and inhale deeply, hoping to suck in her perfume or the scent of that silky hair directly in front of his face, close enough to caress. He preferred women who were out alone, but occasionally followed those who were with a girlfriend or two. He was more careful, then, however – more eyes to catch onto him. He never followed women who were with a boyfriend or husband, though. It was not so much that he felt a threat there; it was simply too frustrating, too painful, to see the woman he thirsted for holding hands with another man, smiling at him, sharing her life with him, and gifting not just his eyes but his hands and his body with her beauty.

After these excursions to the colorful, bustling, electrically alive mall, Lew would return home, a thirty minute ride to his unremarkable little town, to a woodsy rural road, where his small house stood atop a slope reached by a steep driveway that could be a bitch to climb when it had snowed, leveling off where it curved around to his back door. Inside the privacy of this little house, he would open the parcel of his memories like something he had bought at the mall, unpacking all the impressions he had gathered and imprinted, and he would excite himself. Find release. For tonight, anyway.

Eventually, he trailed a few women even into the parking lot, pretending that he couldn't find his car in all the rows of vehicles. And once, he had actually followed a woman in his car as hers left the mall's lot and moved onto the highway, if only for a short distance before she turned off an exit and he kept on going straight toward home.

Today, again on a Saturday, he trawled the mall for someone who would particularly catch his interest. The anticipation of finding a subject was almost more exciting than once he had singled her out.

It had been early evening when he arrived, already dark, because he'd been listless and unmotivated that afternoon, lying in bed feeling oddly spent, his mind oddly emptied, just staring up at the blank ceiling for what seemed hours. But his restlessness, his hunger, had finally compelled him to get up, to shower, to venture outside.

It had snowed the day before, but the roads were well plowed by now, as was the mall's parking lot. However, he had parked right alongside a car that hadn't been cleared of Friday's snow, looking as though it lay under a shroud. Like a giant egg with a pristine, unbroken shell. Its glaring whiteness had disturbed him for a moment. It reminded him of the blank ceiling of his bedroom, that he had been staring at for half the day.

Anyway, now here he was, out of the dark and cold, and inside this place of brightness and life, of glittering products and dazzling promises.

In his wandering through the mall, he would lower his eyes guiltily whenever he passed security guards, who shuffled like manatees that had been squeezed into uniforms and taught to act bipedal, but none of them had ever questioned him despite his frequent mall visits. He supposed he was too inconsequential a creature for even them to notice.

Then, he saw her, and when he did his heart bucked as if sparked with recognition. Or at least, recognition of the type of woman he favored. She was just coming out of a candle store, though with no shopping bag in hand, and he instantly fell into step behind her. The aromatic smell from the candle shop had seemed to announce her appearance, seemed to come from *her*, too intensely pleasurable, making him feel almost giddy. He followed her as she continued along.

Actually, Lew realized, despite his initial impression of her, she was not exactly the type he normally responded to. Yes, she had blond hair — corn silk blond, and shimmering, so long it fell to the small of her back. But he preferred women with curves, sometimes even those who tended a bit toward what was commonly thought of as overweight, considering them ripe and sensual, just as people in earlier times had done. This young woman appeared to be thin, a bit lost in her clothes. Her bottom certainly didn't fill out her jeans in the way he typically liked. He had only had a glimpse of her face before she turned away and started walking, but he'd seen distinct cheekbones. And yet, there had been that mysterious spark, and he trusted it, so he continued trailing her.

She wore a long-sleeved blouse, white with a pattern of large red stars. It was vaguely familiar. Maybe he had seen women in the mall wearing the same blouse before, or even one of the faceless or headless mannequins in the window displays. It was scoop-necked, baring one of her shoulders. Her skin was extremely pale, almost as white as the blouse, and her shoulder was bony. But he wasn't deterred from shadowing her.

She turned into a narrow side corridor that led to some restrooms. He turned into it, too. At its end, she disappeared into the ladies' room. He lingered in the corridor, pretending to check his cell phone. The ladies' room door squealed open and he couldn't stop himself from looking up alertly, but it was another woman, and he returned to his bogus phone scrutiny.

The door creaked again, he looked up, and there she was, walking toward him, though her gaze was fixed straight ahead as if he were invisible.

Seeing her head-on, Lew was startled by just how thin she really was. Her face was gaunt enough to make him imagine that her body must look emaciated, like that of an anorexic. Surely her ribs stood out sharply, her pelvis threatening to tear through rice paper skin. Not only were her cheekbones distinct, but her eyes were recessed in deep cups of bone, her lips thin and colorless, strands of that wispy blond hair hanging down across her face. Her blue eyes looked clouded.

She couldn't be well. Did she indeed suffer from anorexia nervosa, or was she a methamphetamine addict? Though he estimated she was in her early twenties, which was his preference, she had the aspect of someone much older.

So why did he follow in her wake, a few moments after she had walked right past him without acknowledging his existence? Why was his interest in her not eroded one whit, even though her thinness had shocked him? He couldn't even understand, himself, why he was still so gravitated to her. Would he even want to go to bed with such an unhealthy-looking person? Maybe it was this strange, niggling sense of familiarity. And yet, if that was it, who could she possibly remind him of? No one from his past occurred to him. It wasn't as though he'd had that many lovers in his life.

Like a sleepwalker, someone in a fugue state, she was headed toward one of the Southern Cross Mall's multiple entrances/exits. She had no coat to pull on over that white blouse with the red stars. Lew pushed his way outside after her, but he had on his winter coat and he zipped it.

She cut across the parking lot, and in fact was moving in the direction of his own car. Just as it seemed his car truly was her destination – this inexplicable thought causing his heart to judder – she stopped outside the car parked beside his: the car shrouded completely in snow. She reached into the pocket of her baggy jeans, pulled out a set of keys, and inserted one into the driver's side door. She opened the door, and a small amount of snow fell down in the process. Heedless to this, she slipped in behind the wheel and shut the door. Enclosed out of sight.

A moment later, he heard her engine start up. Was she going to get the heat going before she broke out a brush to sweep off her windshield and windows?

Lew let himself into his own car, started his own engine and heat, then lifted his phone into view and again pantomimed that he was reading its little blue screen, while out of the corner of his eye he watched for the blond woman to reemerge from her vehicle. He wondered if he dared offer to clean her windows for her...if he dared break through the wall between himself and the women he followed, at last.

Then, her car started forward. Lew looked directly at it, stunned, forgetting the pretense of his phone. But she hadn't cleared off any of the windows, not even the windshield! She couldn't possibly see. Surely she was on drugs, not in her right state of mind. Surely her car would crash into a parked car or light pole at any moment.

Somehow, though, it didn't, and the snow-cloaked car headed for the parking lot's far exit, and the access road that connected up with the highway.

Lew went in pursuit, closed the distance between them until she was only one car length ahead. As she picked up speed and entered the highway, snow billowed up off her car and swept over his with a hiss. He activated his wipers to brush it aside.

No one driving alongside her car honked at her to alert or chastise her; no one appeared to take any special notice at all. Lew could only gape in disbelief, as they continued on and on, for nearly thirty minutes, until at last her right blinker came on, a mere red smudge under crusted snow. She was taking the same exit that he would normally take coming back from the mall. He trailed her off the highway, and eventually onto a narrow road flanked by snow-frosted evergreens. Deeper into this rural area the two of them advanced, so close that it was as though her car towed his. Her obscured headlights barely glowed upon the road ahead of her, and his own mostly just blazed back at him, reflected from her car's coating of snow.

She took a few off-branching roads, each one a little narrower and more densely wooded than the last. Houses became a little more widely spaced apart. These were the roads he himself would take, coming home.

His heart started juddering again. They had turned onto the road he lived on.

On the right side of the road, the land slipped away precipitously, down to a dark pond with an old mill built beside it. On the left side of the street was a steep slope, all but vertical, with radically angled driveways leading up to the tree-screened houses perched atop it. The snow-crusted car slowed, put on its left blinker, and started climbing one of these driveways.

It was his driveway.

Lew's car hesitated there in the middle of the road, idling, as he watched incredulously. The car ascended his driveway, curving with it toward the summit where things grew level, until the blond woman's vehicle was lost to sight behind his house.

For the first time, he was afraid to continue pursuing her. So she had not been unaware of his attention, after all. Yet, in preceding him, how had she known that this was the home of the man who had been trailing her? Or was it that, throughout his growing number of mall visits lately, she had been following *him*? And now, having baited him into the reverse, was she ready to reveal this? Then what? Did she mean to confront him about his actions...accuse him?

He didn't realize another car had been waiting behind him until he heard it honk impatiently. Startled, he turned into his driveway and started ascending it, himself. What else could he do? This was where he lived. As much as he dreaded speaking with this woman, the invisible wall between them having been exploded, it seemed he had no choice.

His car reached the plateau-like area, thickly hemmed in by trees, where the driveway ended and his small house crouched. The stark beams of his headlights revealed that the blond woman's car was not sitting at the head of his driveway as he had expected to find it, still impossibly blinded by snow. There was no other vehicle at all, and no other way down from his tiny patch of property. No other way through the ring of trees that afforded his home such privacy.

Lew was reluctant to leave his car, and sat there with its motor running as when he had hesitated in the road below. He switched his gaze from the empty spot where he had expected to see the snow-shrouded car, to his house itself. With its windows dark behind its drawn shades, and no outside light left on, it seemed preternaturally silent. But why shouldn't it? He lived alone, and he was here, not in there. No one was in there. Wasn't that right?

The skeletal blond woman could not possibly be inside waiting for him. Could not possibly be lying in the same bed he had lain in for hours earlier, before heading out to the mall. Because, again, where would her car be hidden? Unless…unless it hadn't left the mall's parking lot, after all. Unless it was still sitting there where he had parked alongside it. Where the snowstorm had buried it Friday night.

He kept on just sitting there in his car, gripping its wheel too tightly, too afraid to go to his back door and let himself inside…even though all he wanted now was to lie in his bed again, empty his mind again, stare at the calming blank ceiling. Because the ceiling was so white, so pure. Unlike the walls, and the floor, and the sheets on the bed, which were covered in red constellations, splattered with red stars.

BLUE MANNEQUINS

They gather in the rubble strewn lot between two shattered buildings, those blue mannequins that survive from a different age, maybe the past or maybe the future, stepping out of the caves blasted into the sides of the shattered buildings, a powdering of plaster dust on their smooth blue bodies, mannequins made of sky blue porcelain, jointed with glints of brass. All the surfaces of their jointed bodies are engraved with debossed designs, designs like vines crawling and twining across the blue porcelain, debossed vines filled with gold that has flaked in places just as the porcelain has chipped and cracked, delicate cracks like designs entwined with the vines, from the passage of years either stretching ahead or stretching behind.

They step lightly over the blasted rubble with blind grace, the robin's egg blue mannequins of an earlier or later age, gathering in the lot between the blasted buildings, and boys and girls in tattered clothes have mounted to the upper floors, peering down from empty windows, watching furtively as the beautiful robin's egg blue mannequins assemble and begin the dance they do at every dusk, slow motion pirouettes and slow graceful arm gestures that tell unspoken stories of long ago or future ages, these mannequins with blank faces who do not glimpse the hidden boys and girls, who have no mouths to sing their secret songs of times to come or times so old, just blank faces of swirling vines filled with gold.

The boys and girls with masks of caked dirt and tattered clothing ache at the beauty of the blue blue mannequins, yearn to be as beautiful as they, and to know of distant times they were not yet alive to see or will not live to see, and dream of joining in the dance of the blue blue mannequins that gather in the vacant lot at every dusk, assemble between the two blasted buildings to silently twirl and wave their vine entwined limbs of blue blue porcelain jointed with glimmers of brass, these premonitions of the future or souvenirs of the past.

The children hide though the dancing mannequins cannot see them, they do not go down to the lot due to awe and the fear that they will disrupt the dance of the sky blue mannequins, but they sing even though the mannequins have no ears to hear them, sing the only 500 words they have learned, to supply the words to the unheard music the mannequins dance to. The children in their tattered clothes watching the mannequins from the high empty windows of the two blasted buildings do not know the origin of the sky blue mannequins, but they know 500 words, 500 words are all that they know, and every evening at dusk when the mannequins gather in the vacant lot of rubble to enact their graceful dance the dirty-faced children call down their song like twilight birds, the only song they know or have heard, their song of 500 words. 500 words.

THE CONVERGENCE

For how many centuries had certain secretive, dark-hearted human beings attempted to summon the Vastest into the world, to destroy and recreate it as Its own? They had etched diagrams in the dirt at the center of rings of standing stones, painted complex overlapping symbols in blood on wooden floors with candles set at various nodal points, had drawn complicated geometric patterns into the corners of oddly-angled attic rooms. However, even the greatest adepts had only managed to conjure a portal giving them a limited view into another realm – the realm in which the Vastest was imprisoned – or else, at best, had summoned one of the Lesser Vast.

But there was a cemetery in the town of Eastborough, Massachusetts where a convergence occurred solely by chance. It was a remarkable occurrence, as remarkable as if the earth had coughed up the perfectly formed tiny gears, mainspring, escapement, and balance wheel of a watch's mechanism, and joined them together in absolute harmony with each other, purely by dumb luck. But hadn't something of that kind happened before, when molecular evolution had slowly and gradually – but mindlessly – led to the formation of the first living cells?

In this cemetery there was an eighteenth century gravestone bearing the image of a man wearing a wig, so it would seem, of curls, with ungainly stone angel wings in place of a body. His epitaph read:

> Here is deposited the Remains
> of Mr Samuel Cowan
> Died June 24 1775
> in the 81 Year
> of his Age
>
> Here lies deposited his remains
> He was beloved by his acquaintances
> for his many amiable virtues. He
> is lamented by those who in him
> have lost an example of meekness
> and unaffected piety. The righteous
> are taken from the evil to come.

This gravestone was thoroughly spotted with the symbiotic composite organism called lichen, itself a kind of convergence, these ugly patches like the lesions of a plague. It so happened that one of these lichen patches – accidentally having formed a perfect circle – had grown over a shallow crack near the base of the listing gravestone on its front side, close to the earth. The crack diagonally, and only by random design, split this circle of lichen into two precisely equal halves.

So had this combination of features remained for many years, such an unremarkable detail in a cemetery filled with gravestones marred by cracks and lichen that not even the most ardent gravestone rubbing aficionado would have taken note of it. But, one summer a lawnmower operated by a groundskeeper spat out a clod of grass that stuck to the face of Samuel Cowan's gravestone, very near to the circle of lichen, so that several of the blades of grass lay across the lichen circle and the crack like drawn lines, intersecting the diagonal fissure at several different angles. The clod of earth remained stuck there, and the grass blades dried yellow in the sun. Still, weeks went by without anything at all remarkable taking place.

And it would have remained that way, had not an ant crawled upon the surface of Samuel Cowan's gravestone. Even so, had it been another type of ant – smaller, or red instead of black – the event would never have become notable. The most critical factor, however, was that this ant had five legs instead of six, having lost one leg in a confrontation with a beetle. That this ant had only five legs made all the difference in meshing the delicate gears of this chance mechanism.

For no particular reason, beyond the unreasoning mechanical behavior of ants, the five-legged creature crawled up from a blade of grass onto the face of the gravestone of Samuel Cowan, and entered that circle of lichen like a necromancer stepping into the center of his pentagram. The ant crossed the intersected lines caused by the crack and the dried yellow grass blades.

And then, in the nucleus of this configuration, the ant became transfixed as if pinned to the spot. It went from black to glowing green. A luminous green web of force spread out rapidly from the ant...across the entire surface of the gravestone...across the ground throughout the cemetery, then beyond the cemetery, pouring over every surface vertical or horizontal...up the trees and across the houses that lined the streets of Eastborough, Massachusetts...sweeping over the cars driving its streets and the people walking its sidewalks, transfixing them, too...making them, too, glow entirely green.

And when all the green strands of this web joined together into a wholeness, a solid greenness, this manifestation was the Vastest. The Vastest was *all*. And the world before the summoning of the Vastest, and before the five-legged ant, and the clump of grass, and the crack in stone, and the spot of lichen, and the erection of the gravestone, and the life and death of Samuel Cowan, was ended.

CRACKED LIPS

New York City, 1850

After having sought contact from the inventor Joseph Faber for several months, to no avail, word finally came back to Schenkel that Faber was dead — by his own hand. The news affected Schenkel deeply on two counts. For one, he had wanted Faber to make some repairs to the Euphonia machine he had designed specifically for Schenkel, at the latter's great expense. And the other aspect of this news that distressed Schenkel was that his dear wife Eva had also died by her own hand, three years earlier. It was Eva's suicide, of course, that had been behind Schenkel having approached Faber in the first place.

Still absorbing the news, Schenkel wandered into his parlor, which — as he had received few visitors since Eva's death — was given over entirely to the Euphonia. It was P. T. Barnum who had dubbed Faber's "talking machine" with that name, when the crafty showman had begun exhibiting it to a public that had ultimately proved ignorant and unimpressed. Schenkel, though, had been only too impressed with the work of his fellow German. Having heard of the machine, and since Faber had also settled in New York City, Schenkel had brought the inventor to his home to create a Euphonia machine of his very own. It was in critical ways unlike the one shown by Barnum. This one had been meant to perform for Schenkel alone.

All other furnishings had been removed from the parlor. Schenkel had even had his servants remove the paintings from the walls, and the large mirror that had been mounted above the mantelpiece. This hadn't been based on Faber's recommendations, but was his own inspiration. Schenkel wanted nothing in this room to distract his focus from the machine that stood in the center of the bare wooden floor.

"Poor bedeviled man," Schenkel said aloud in German, as he stood now in front of the Euphonia. In front of the machine's human face. "He finally gave in to his despair. The common fools could not appreciate his brilliance. If only he could have maintained hope, and carried on longer...not allow himself to slip beneath the dark waters." He stared at the artificial countenance set into the machine. Not on the far side, as in Faber's Euphonia, but situated directly above the keyboard, so that Schenkel could look into its painted glass eyes when he sat at those keys. His voice hitched as he continued, "If only you could have stopped yourself from slipping beneath those black waters yourself, my love. If only *I* could have stopped you."

He sat down on the cushioned bench in front of the machine's seventeen piano-like keys. One of these labeled keys operated a mechanism analogous with the human glottis, while the other sixteen produced all the principle sounds that were required to approximate human speech. A foot pedal pumped a large black bellows behind the mounted mask, so that the vocal sounds – and something like breath, gusting gently in Schenkel's face whenever the Euphonia spoke to him – issued from its movable lips of India rubber.

Oh, the hours that Faber had worked in this room, perfecting the machine, fine-tuning the complex collection of reeds and whistles...of levers and cords that stood in for muscles and tendons...the movement of the jaw and tongue within the molded rubber mask. Fine-tuning all those intricate mechanisms until Faber had replicated, inasmuch as possible, and to Schenkel's obsessive specifications, the sound of his precious Eva's voice. Just as Faber had worked diligently, in collaboration with several artists, to create a visage that resembled with uncanny accuracy the features of Schenkel's beautiful young bride, framed in a curly blond wig of real human hair.

In the beginning, when he was alone with the Euphonia – with Eva – Schenkel would sit at the keyboard and speak to the mask, ask it questions such as, "You did love me, didn't you, my darling?"

Then, at first with agonizing slowness...until, as the months passed, his fingers grew more swift and adept, and the machine's utterances came less haltingly...he would type Eva's own answers for her. In its soft and unearthly monotone, the mask would move its lips and reply, "Of course I loved you, my dear husband. With all my heart."

"And you did know happiness with me?"

"Oh yes, Daniel, you know I did!"

Schenkel would give a loud sob, then, and with tears blurring the face hovering before him – making it seem all the more pliable and lifelike – he would weep, "So then, was it my doubt that caused you to do what you did, my love? Was it my accusations? My cruel distrust?"

"No...no, my love. You mustn't blame yourself," Eva would reassure him. "I suffered these dark moods all my life. I hinted as much to you. It was my nature, darling Daniel...only my own nature."

But how many times had he begged this reassurance from her? Finding only fleeting comfort in the words that he himself put in her mouth, before he needed to ask her – ask himself – the same questions again?

After two years these words of reassurance, even coming from Eva's face, in Eva's voice, brought him less and less solace...until he had come upon another way in which to use the Euphonia, purely by chance. He doubted that Faber, a man of science, would have believed him or even approve. No, it wasn't to show Faber his new technique that Schenkel had wanted to bring the man back to his home. His reason was that over time, with the mask's oft-repeated movements, and drying out as rubber will do, Eva's face had begun to crack around the jaw and lips, its paint to blister and flake. Schenkel had hoped Faber would replace or somehow repair the mask. Now, with the man dead, Schenkel was left only with the possibility of tracking down the artists with whom Faber had collaborated when fashioning the mask originally.

Schenkel had not intended to relate to Faber the story of how late one night, after the servants had retired, and having imbibed too many glasses of whiskey, he had found himself seated in front of the Euphonia and crying out aloud, "If you loved me as you say, how could you do this thing to me? How could you leave me this way, Eva?" Then he had thrown his head down low over the keys, and with eyes squeezed tightly shut, in a fit of anguish, had played at the keys blindly and wildly, like a piano virtuoso in a fever of inspiration.

And as a result, Eva's words had come.

"If you loved me as much as you claimed, Daniel, how could you accuse me of taking other men to my bed when you were away? Your friends, and even our servants?"

Schenkel had snapped upright then, his eyes gone wide, and in jerking away from the keyboard, away from Eva's unblinking white face, had toppled backward off the piano bench and crashed onto his back on the floor.

His servants had come running at the sound, alarmed. They said they had heard him quarreling with someone, and had thought an intruder had attacked him. By then he was back on his feet, however, and he sent them away brusquely. When he was once again alone, he turned to face Eva again. Silently staring Eva, still beautiful even with the webs of cracks around her jaw and the fissures splitting her plump lips.

"I'm sorry, my darling," he whispered to her. "Forgive me, Eva. Please...can you forgive me?"

Tentatively, he reseated himself. Gingerly, placed his fingers on the keys once more. But the shock had partly sobered him, and his eyes were open, and his intentions too deliberate. Even when he tried depressing the keys at random, without any conscious intent, he produced only disturbing gibberish in place of coherent words. Finally, these sounds unsettled him so greatly that he had to stop.

But over the weeks and months that followed, he had tried further experimentation, and had been met with occasional success. The formula seemed to be some mysterious combination of tears and whiskey...whereby he entered into a state of mind frantic and tormented enough to summon forth Eva's spirit, enabling it to speak through the Euphonia, if only very briefly.

Oh, of course he questioned what was taking place. Hadn't he in the past visited spiritualists in an attempt to contact Eva by means of séance, only to be tricked by charlatans and their darkness-concealed assistants? He had even consulted a Chinese spiritualist, who had employed a technique called *fuji*, whereby a planchette traced symbols in the spread ashes of burnt incense. Supposedly Eva had delivered a few enigmatic words to Schenkel in that manner, but he had distrusted the spiritualist...had suspected that the man was either seeking to delude him, or actually believed in the spirit writing but was only deluding himself.

So once again, couldn't it be that it was merely Schenkel's own mind that was ascribing these utterances to Eva, yet this time unconsciously? Deep down, though, he felt that wasn't the case. Because where once Eva would have only reassured him, now when the mask's lips moved the words that came through them were quite different in tone. *Accusing* in tone, as he had once accused her.

"Oh, if only you had believed in me, Daniel, everything would have been so different. But I couldn't stand your horrid words any longer...all your doubt in my character. All your doubt in my love."

There were times when, after such sessions, Schenkel swore to never sit at the Euphonia again. He couldn't bring himself to destroy it, but he would cover it with a great cloth and lock the parlor up. Only days later, however, he would be unlocking that door again. Drawing away that white shroud. He would lean in, as if to apologize for his absence, and kiss Eva's cracked lips. Where once he would only kiss them lightly, he would now kiss them lingeringly. Would push his tongue into her mouth, and play it across her own wooden tongue. And then he would start pouring the whiskey, and pouring the tears.

Now, still brooding on Faber's suicide, and finding himself empathizing with the poor man's misery to an uncomfortable extent, Schenkel said to Eva, "I can understand why he could no longer bear to live, with people accusing him of trickery, mocking him, and failing to realize how important his work might become. I can understand your frustrations, too, my dear...oh yes, you must believe me. You both suffered unfairly. Life is unending pain, is it not? I don't even know why I continue, when I have lost the only thing that was truly important to me. In this light, can't you understand my doubts and insecurities? It was only because I loved you so very, very much. Only because my greatest fear was losing you. And in fearing such, I fulfilled those very fears!"

Schenkel didn't touch the keys, to seek an answer to his questions or a response to his statements. He wasn't ready yet. He rose from the bench, and turned to the cold fireplace behind him. From its mantelpiece he took down the only other features remaining in the parlor: a bottle of whiskey and a glass, tipping the former into the latter. He drank down a generous portion in one gulp before turning back to the Euphonia.

"If I had the courage, I would join you. But do I deserve it? Have I earned my place beside you again? What must I do to atone, my love?"

He drank down more whiskey. Asked more questions without sitting down at the keyboard for his answers. He walked the bare floor, around the Euphonia as if in its orbit, around and around, as if he couldn't find his way out of the room.

Finally, though, when there was enough drink in him and his eyes had filled up, he set the glass aside and seated himself on the bench. He spread his trembling fingers above the keys, not yet touching them.

"What is it like where you are, darling? Tell me!"

Then, with eyes crunched shut he crashed his fingers down on the keys, fingers flickering madly, side to side.

The flat, distant voice through the cracked rubber lips sighed, "It is cold and empty where I am."

"Oh, my Eva!" Schenkel blurted, juddering with sobs. "It is just as cold and empty here, because I am without you! It is Hell here – *Hell!* But is there a Hell? Is there a Heaven? I need to know where to find you when the time comes that I am worthy. Tell me, Eva...tell me...where are you now?"

"I am standing behind you."

Schenkel whirled around on the cushioned bench, and met Eva's fixed eyes, dark in her pallid face. His first thought was that the mask set into the Euphonia was reflected in the mirror over the mantelpiece.

But then he remembered that he had had the servants remove the mirror from the wall.

***

Those servants would later relate that they had found their master dead, still seated at the Euphonia, his forehead resting on the keys, his grieving heart having apparently given out. Perhaps it was his head having dropped to the keys of that strange machine of his, expending the last of the air in the bellows, that had caused the strange sound that had brought the servants running to investigate. Even though they had heard many a strange sound come from the closed parlor before, this one had been exceptionally uncanny.

It had sounded, they swore, like a woman's loud, long wail of sorrow.

ALWAYS

They had a break every four hours, and they chose to think of one break as breakfast, the next as lunch. The cafeteria was on the floor above them, so at what they considered first break they would leave their work area together, make a stop at the restrooms, then cross the vast manufacturing floor, find their way out into the spacious central stairwell, and ascend to the fourth level. Because it made them feel bonded, they liked to eat and drink identical things, so they'd both get the same kind of coffee: either a large black ice coffee (in a double cup, since one paper cup would get too soggy over several hours) or a black hot coffee, preferably flavored, depending on what had been set out in decanters. Then a pastry, usually a doughnut. He teased her about her love of doughnuts, and pretended to blame her for causing his belly to grow fatter, although in reality neither of them would ever grow fatter.

They paid the cashier with a debit card that never ran out of funds, because they never ran out of work.

They would return to their floor, their department, and take break standing up at their station. They never brought

42

chairs into their work area, though they were permitted to. He said sitting down sapped his energy, made him too lazy, and he'd held stand-up jobs all his life. Because he felt this way, she simply followed suit. She always stood to the left, just as she had always used to sleep on the left side of their bed. It was unthinkable to them that they would alter this arrangement. Being spouses was about ritual.

They'd set their breakfast coffees down on the blue vinyl antistatic mat upon which they assembled and disassembled disk drives, and play on their computer together for the duration of their break while they munched their doughnuts. Their computer privileges were limited; they could not send emails, post personal updates or comments on social media, contact or communicate with the outside world at all, really. Acting purely as spectators, though, they could monitor the daily news outside the company, enter subjects of interest into search engines, read fiction published online, and pursue their favorite activity: visit video sharing websites.

It was on one of these sites that they had built several video playlists that ran in the background as a personal soundtrack while they worked. They had both contributed to these. Though they favored love songs to foster a soothing, mellow mood, he was older than her, so he had added a good many pop hits from the 70s – not always because he admired their artistry (the sappier the better, sometimes), but for their nostalgia value. *Make Love Stay* (Dan Fogelberg), *Fool (If You Think It's Over)* (Chris Rea), *On and On* (Stephen Bishop), *A Dream Goes On Forever* (Todd Rundgren). She tended toward songs from the 80s and 90s: *I'll Always Love You* (Taylor Dane), *Don't Dream It's Over* (Crowded House), *Always and Forever* (Luther

Vandross), *I Don't Want to Live Without You* (Foreigner), *Always* (Atlantic Starr). *Always* was the song they had danced to at their wedding.

Some of these tender songs were all the more poignant because the artist was dead. Fogelberg and Vandross for sure. Others must be passing away as time continued on, but they just hadn't learned about it.

Sometimes to poke each other, because it seemed as though half of their interaction while working was to playfully tease, they would sneak songs the other disliked into each other's playlist when one of them went off to the restroom alone, and then wait for that song to come up eventually while they worked. They both liked hiding Rick Astley's *Together Forever* in each other's playlists...though actually they didn't hate that song, had only ever been afraid to admit that they liked it.

They had met on the job, at another company all but identical with this one. Having been with that company longer than she, he had trained her how to disassemble disk drives that had finished testing, so that their three main components could be dispersed to manufacturing: the disk drive itself (in its free state, called a raw drive), the little circuit board that helped the drive communicate with a data storage cabinet (called a paddle card), and the frame (dubbed a drive carrier) that held them together and enabled an assembled drive to be fitted into said cabinet. They had recorded every component and every transaction into their shared computer back then, and still did so now.

In this place, which mostly replicated the company in which they had met and continued working after their marriage, their duties were similar to before, yet different.

He still broke down assembled drives and boxed up their individual parts, stacking these boxes onto wooden pallets, shrink-wrapping them, then using a handcart to transport them to the elevator, down to the first floor, and to the warehouse.

Her function was to take a handcart down in the elevator to the first floor, find shrink-wrapped pallets of drive parts, bring them up to the third floor and their work area, cut away the shrink wrap, slice open the boxes, remove the individual parts, and assemble them into finished disk drives.

For her husband to disassemble.

***

At lunch break they often chose a hamburger or a chicken sandwich, though the latter might be dried out if it had sat under the lamp too long. Maybe a salad from the salad bar instead; there was more variety to be had there. Coffee again. They would take their food down to their work station just as they did at first break. They didn't eat at the cafeteria tables with other workers, though in the beginning they'd been invited. Generally they kept to themselves, except for a few people they chatted with occasionally in the vicinity of their own work area. Because she had been quite attractive in life, younger than him, a fair number of times when she hadn't been with her husband – maybe on her way to the restroom, or the warehouse – men in nice clothes from one of the offices or more informally attired from one of the production areas had invited her upstairs to lunch or to have a coffee, or had simply flirted with her, not aware in the beginning that she was married. She had politely declined every offer, and when she would tell her husband about it later he wouldn't get too jealous. Not too. He didn't doubt her commitment to him. That was why they had been bound to each other in this way.

Did those men who found her attractive fantasize about sneaking her away to some quiet corner of this great structure, in which they were contained without possibility of exit, so as to make love with her? Did any of the other inhabitants of this building do such things? She and her husband had never dared, because they knew it was against the rules, and their greatest fear was being punished by being separated from each other. It couldn't be risked. They were all they had, and all they wanted.

Well that wasn't entirely true. Just as being inseparable was their eternal reward, they were simultaneously being punished as well, because things weren't as black and white as they had been led to believe in life. He had been married once before, and had a son who was autistic, twenty-two but very childlike. As they worked side-by-side he would tell his wife stories about his son's early years, long before she had met her husband, and in the telling he would miss his gentle son with such stabbing intensity that he would break into tears. She would hold him then. Their work area was largely shielded by pallets of boxes, so they weren't afraid of hugs and brief kisses.

He would never see his son again. That was a punishment; it had to be. But if his son had been in the car with them that morning, on that icy trip to work, would he now be here beside them, too? Would he join them at a much later date, perhaps as a very old man, older looking than his father? He still didn't understand all the mechanics of these matters, despite what his coworkers shared about their own situations. Each person had their own reason for being here, specifically.

He could only hope his son, who took things in stride in his easy accepting way, wasn't missing him too badly in turn. Still blissfully played his videogames, still laughed at his favorite videos on the same video sharing site that his father and stepmother favored, watching them over and over and over. Being autistic, he found comfort and harmony in routine.

His son lived with his mother. He was grateful his son still had her.

His wife would sometimes kiss the tears from the corners of his eyes, joking with him that they tasted of all the coffee he drank, making him laugh, and he would be reminded of the reward again, not the punishment, and the blade of pain would be sheathed once more – until the next time it appeared. Everything happened in cycles. But there was a kind of comfort and harmony in that, too.

***

Sometimes they'd yawn sleepily – around the time of first break, when it came along four hours after second break – as if they were still in the process of fully waking up for the day. But it was only a kind of programming, or conditioning, because it had been a long time since they had lain together. That was what she missed most of all. She felt it was a punishment that had been geared especially for her. She missed lying curled tight against his body, warm under a thick quilt. Once, early on, she had spread some sheets of cardboard on the floor under their work table and convinced him to lie down upon them with her, just to cuddle, and maybe to nap for the duration of their lunch break (although they never really felt the need for sleep), but one of their coworkers happening past had spotted them, laughed loudly, and asked them what they thought they were doing. They had never risked it again, lest they be discovered by their manager, who was very kind and mild but still a manager — perhaps not even a man — and he might report them to his superiors and cause them to be punished in a worse way.

They were here to enact one scenario. They kept their hands busy, and learned to be grateful for what they had. And that was each other. But that didn't prevent the cycle of tears.

On the morning of the accident, still not long married, they had showered together. This had led to amorous feelings that had continued when they began dressing. Soon they were undressing again, and moving back to the bedroom. Their lovemaking had caused them to be late for work. How many times had he berated himself for that, and begged her forgiveness? But she always reassured him that she hadn't noticed him driving too fast to make up for the lost time.

So now, his right forearm forever smelled of her deodorant, smeared into his skin when he had wrapped his arm around her. His facial hair always smelled of her juices. The smell wouldn't wash off even when he splashed cold water in his face at the sink in the men's room — not that he wanted to wash the scent off, because surely he didn't. He was grateful for it. Though it seemed a tease, a taunting reminder of things lost and denied, he chose to think of it as part of the gift they had been given; a lasting remembrance.

But she was crying again now, and stopped assembling her disk drives, because they had been talking suggestively to each other, joking around flirtingly as they often did. At one point he had accidentally dropped his pen to the floor, and she had told him that the next time he bent over she was going to fuck him in the ass. With a deadpan expression, he had immediately knocked his pen on the floor again. She had started laughing, but the laughter had turned into hard sobs. She wept because they would never make love again. So he folded his arms around her, kissed her ear through her hair and comforted her, while keeping one eye out for their manager.

She went to the restroom then, to wash her face and compose herself a little, and grab a cup of cold water. She brought one back for him, too.

A little while later, when the Atlantic Starr song in their favorite playlist had finished, Rick Astley began singing *Together Forever.*

She slapped her husband's arm, and laughed.

CARNY GODDESS

There was a racetrack on Route 9 when I was a kid, right here in my hometown of Eastborough, Massachusetts – called the Eastborough Speedway, in fact – and on summer nights even from my yard you could hear the distant car engines rumbling. In my lush, overgrown yard, on a humid summer's night, I liked to pretend I was listening to the growls of dinosaurs. My father always told me I had an excess of imagination. I thought I just had a keen sense of wonder. I think that's essential in a child. It may be the only time in our lives when we aren't blind.

Dinosaurs. Fitting, really. The speedway has long since been a shopping plaza, and I never did see even one of its races, but for a week every summer its grounds were host to an attraction that interested me far more. It was a traveling carnival, the particular name of which – if it ever had one – I never knew.

Was it every summer? No...I recall now that some years it was a week in spring. Sometimes the carnival would stay for a couple of weeks. Some years, to my great disappointment, it didn't come at all.

When it did come my father never failed to bring me, and usually his brother would accompany us – along with my cousin Bill, who was two years younger than me. The men tended to leave us to pursue their own pleasures, though. There was a beer garden, and a girlie show. That was something I never caught even one time, either.

But Bill and I would steal looks at this midway strip show from a distance, not really understanding what went on inside, not yet understanding the dirty-feeling curiosity that drew us to its outer orbit. One time, one of the scantily clad ladies up on the bally – as the little stage outside the sideshow tents was called – caught my eye over the balding heads of my own and other kids' fathers, and winked at me. My heart's clapper rang against its sides. She wasn't a sleazy performer to my ten-year-old mind, but a princess on a pedestal in her 60s big bleached hair and her boa-lined red negligee.

Talk about a sense of wonder. Even before ten I was under the disorienting, the distorting spell of the fairer sex. I remember betting my sister's friends that I was strong enough to pick them up. Talk about a pick-up line. Well, it was as good a way as any for an eight-year-old to get his arms around a beguiling twelve-year-old older woman. A precursor, though I didn't know it then, to the amorous exertions of adulthood. But would women ever again be as magical to me as they had been back then?

The same year the woman in red negligee winked at me, Bill and I saw another female carnival worker die. In a way.

There was a trapeze act – a modest setup, outside of any tent. A placard posted the times the aerialists would perform. During the afternoon Bill and I saw them performing from afar, and we'd meant to catch a later show but then forgot until it was too late to claim a good vantage point. By the time we did approach the act, brightly lit under night's black sky, there was already a crowd so thick we could barely penetrate its edge. Standing on tiptoes and craning our necks did little to improve our view. Had we not been close to the setup earlier, between acts, we wouldn't have known that there was no safety net stretched below the trapeze framework.

Off to the side there was a trailer, and from it emerged the acrobats the crowd had gathered for. I had a less obscured view of the trailer, and so I could see the performers clearly before they approached the trapeze rig. There was a youngish, good-looking man who bounded ahead of the other two trapeze artists to start things off with some solo work. I watched him for a few minutes before my attention was drawn back to the other two. They were an older man who was balding but obviously still in good shape, and a young woman. They wore silvery, glittery outfits, the woman's like a one-piece swimsuit that bared her strong, shapely legs up to the hip. She had honey blond hair tied back in a ponytail. Though to my youthful eye she seemed a full-fledged woman, in retrospect I know she must have only been twenty or so, if not younger.

Was she the balding man's daughter? I didn't think so. He had his arm around her while he smoked a cigarette and watched his companion's act, but his embrace didn't seem paternal to me. Not the way his hand curled around one of her rounded hips, sliding up and down its curve. I should hope he wasn't her father, anyway.

There was discomfort on the young woman's fresh, lovely face as she too watched the younger man perform. It looked almost like fear. But whether it was fear of performing, or of the balding man's affection, I couldn't say even now. Maybe, she was having a sense of foreboding about both situations.

The young woman was so beautiful, she put the earlier goddess out of my mind altogether. That other was more carnal, this woman more ethereal. In her shimmering silver, an angel soon to take flight. She and the balding man now sprang toward the trapeze, the man with a hand on her back as if to push her...to plunge her forward.

They commenced their routine, and I was captivated by the woman's grace, her legs held together and streaming behind her like a comet's tail as she shot through the air. The older man, his legs hooked over his rung, reached upside-down to catch her. He swung her outward, and on the return arc she spun like a ballerina pivoting on thin air, reaching out for her own bar as it swung back to her. She caught it, whooshed outward...far outward.

And then, a snapping sound. I suppose a bolt had come loose, for one of the two cords supporting the bar the woman gripped came loose. The angel fell — plummeted from view, behind the clustered audience. Over their screams and cries, I swear I heard a heavy thud.

"Oh my God, Tom!" my cousin Bill said. "Is she dead? Is she dead?" He grabbed hold of my arm.

"I don't know!" I said, shaking off his grip.

We couldn't get near the scene. The crowd had surged forward. Other carnival workers came running. I stood back and waited to see if the woman would be carried back to her trailer. As I lingered there, feeling sick with dread, a hand clamped onto my shoulder. Startled, I looked around to see my father standing behind me, my uncle beside him. My father's familiar scents of cigarettes and beer wafted over me, grounding me. "What happened, Tom — somebody fell?"

"Yes...a girl," I said.

"Oh no," said my uncle.

"Come on," my father steered me away, "you don't want to see this."

"I want to know if she's okay," I protested, looking back over my shoulder.

"She'll be okay," he assured me. "That's not like a big circus trapeze. I'm sure she's fine."

The trapeze looked high enough to me, but I tried to take heart in my father's words. That is, until a middle-aged woman pushed her way out of the audience, doubled over and vomited onto the dirt.

***

A year later, the carnival never showed up in the summer, but it did come unannounced — and for only a single day — in autumn. On October 31st.

The word of it spread through school like a wild rumor, whispered lest too much talk should disperse the reality into mist. On the way to school, several kids had seen the carnival being erected on the speedway grounds. It created a real quandary — if we were to go to the carnival that night, we would have to forego trick-or-treating. Well, it wasn't really that much of a dilemma. I'm sure many homeowners ended up with a lot of extra candy on their hands that night, perplexed by the scanty showing of ghouls in the streets. Most of the kids in Eastborough hounded their parents to let them go to the carnival, instead.

My father took me, as usual, though his brother and Bill – who lived out of town – didn't accompany us, it still being a weeknight. As usual, though, father parked himself in the beer pavilion to chat and smoke with other fathers. Like most of the kids who attended the carnival that night, I opted to wear my Halloween costume, the holiday's magic still being in the crisp, chilly air. Maybe the magic was even heightened beyond the norm. This year, I wore a cheap, brittle plastic glow-in-the-dark skull mask fastened to my head with a rubber band.

The carnival, I found, was decked out for the holiday, too: the aisles of the midway were festooned with strings of fat orange bulbs. Cotton cobwebs were stretched between the trailers and food stands, blown leaves snared in them like the husks of giant spiders.

My favorite attraction was always the haunted house ride, but this year when I approached it I hesitated, as a flurry of teary specters came running out of its exit in a panic, screaming into their bewildered parents' arms. Though I was now eleven-years-old, I couldn't will myself to join the increasingly skittish line to go inside.

Another favorite ride of mine was a double Ferris wheel, the two wheels of which would rotate around each other like the gears of some titan machine. But I saw that it had jammed, moving only a little bit with ear-piercing screeches before it jarred to a halt again, shuddered and shook with futile effort. It was full of people, children wailing on high, their voices ghostly and drifting with the leaves. I didn't know if this were truly accidental, or another enhancement in honor of the season.

Cheated of two of my favorite rides, I drifted on until I saw a gaggle of people gathered around an outdoors live act. I was able to negotiate my way close to the inner barrier this time. It was a knife throwing routine. A man, all in black, and wearing a black mask over his eyes like the Lone Ranger, had already pitched a number of balanced blades toward a woman who stood with her back against a much-perforated wooden board. As he readied for his next throw, the man – who was losing his hair – clamped a cigarette between his thin lips.

I looked toward the woman, and flinched when the knife thunked into the wood above her head and quivered there, continuing an outline of her body. She was a young woman, with long straight blond hair and dreamy-lidded eyes, reminding me of an actress I had a crush on at that time, Peggy Lipton in *The Mod Squad*. Her arms were by her sides, her body rigid...except, oddly, she held her head cocked at a slight angle, giving her a quizzical aspect. Around her throat she wore a black velvet ribbon. Her knife thrower assistant's costume consisted of a one-piece outfit like a bathing suit, scintillating and silver.

My heart jammed to a halt in my chest, shuddered and shook like the double Ferris wheel as it fought to regain its proper rhythm. It couldn't be the same girl I had seen fall from the trapeze a year ago, could it? That girl had had her hair tied back in a ponytail, but if she had let it fall free, wouldn't she have looked like this girl? So, had my father been right after all, and she had survived the accident? If that were the case, maybe she had been grounded ever since, consigned to acts like this one instead. Her face was composed, almost waxen, those sexy dreamy eyes unblinking as they stared back at the knife thrower. Or through him.

Suddenly, as he wound up for another throw, the equally silent knife thrower looked familiar to me, too.

I wasn't sure how it happened. Did a kid call out to his friend too loudly? Did the knife thrower see something distracting out of the corner of his eye? A gust of chilly breeze picked up just then; did it send a shiver through his body at that crucial moment?

Whatever the case, his next throw went wild. The knife thunked home, but this time in the hollow between his mute assistant's collarbones.

Screams. Cries. The girl fell back against the board and slumped down it, her hands fluttering helplessly as if she were too drugged to respond otherwise.

Other carnival workers rushed in, blocked my view for several minutes. The girl's limp body was slung into the air and carried to a nearby trailer.

In a daze, shuffling mindlessly like a zombie in my skull mask, I somehow found my way to my father in the beer garden, and stammered to him what I'd seen. He pushed my muffling mask up on my head and asked me to repeat myself.

"Oh, come on, Tom," he said, clapping me on the arm. "I'm sure that was all staged, just to scare kids like you on Halloween. I've seen all kinds of weird things going on here tonight."

I could hardly argue with that statement, at least.

***

My father took a new job in Worcester, Massachusetts, so my family moved from Eastborough to that city, to a small house on hilly Orient Street. We stopped going to the carnival in Eastborough. Anyway, it didn't arrive that next year – in spring, summer or autumn – and though it did come around the following year, I was now thirteen and my father must have thought it wouldn't be of the same interest to me.

I didn't attend the carnival again until I was seventeen-years-old. I had my driver's license now, and my father had bought me a four-year-old 1970 Javelin. Better than that, I had my first girlfriend – Debbie, a short pretty classmate who strongly resembled Maureen McCormick of *The Brady Bunch*. Oh, but I felt like the luckiest man in Worcester. I decided to take my very own goddess to the carnival in Eastborough that summer, the summer that we both graduated from high school, on one of our first dates.

The double Ferris wheel was functioning properly this time, and at its very summit I put my arm around Debbie's shoulders, drew her against me and planted a kiss on her lips. She giggled and pushed me away. "Tom!" she scolded, but she was grinning. Did she feel as exhilarated as I did, up there with the carnival's constellations of lights spread out below us?

And this year, no one appeared to be fleeing from the haunted house ride in tears. (Well, there was always one or two.) I thought this might be another opportunity for a kiss, a longer kiss, so I pulled Debbie toward it. She kept protesting, shrinking against my body at the gravelly, distorted roars and howls coming from the attraction's loudspeakers, but this only encouraged me more. Even before our car started into motion, Debbie had already shrunk down into her seat against me. It made me grin like the skull mask I'd worn six years earlier.

As our car began to crank along its track to the attraction's entrance, I took note of its operator for the first time. He wore a black hooded cloak, and the glimpse I had of his shadowed face unsettled me for some reason.

I saw the cigarette dangling from the man's mouth for only a second, and then our car banged its nose through the black-painted hinged double doors. It took an immediate jolting left, and we lurched straight into the realm of dark magic. Dark magic as rendered by dry ice, strobe lights and fluorescent paint. Debbie yelped and buried her head into my shoulder as one garish demon after another shot up from behind a gravestone, sat up in a coffin, or dropped down from a hangman's noose. If they were to be dragged outside, their papier-mâché forms would look as pitiful and harmless as vampires desiccated in the sun's light. But here, in their own domain, they had power.

Our car banged into another room, and air blasted our faces as a recorded voice cackled maniacally. Debbie was too scrunched down for me to kiss, but at least I had my arm tightly around her. I looked down at her and laughed, and when I looked up again a spotlight came on to illuminate a ghoul just in front of us. It was a female manikin seated in a moving rocking chair. This figure was far more realistic than the papier-mâché fiends, perhaps a retired department store manikin reduced to this less glamorous profession. The figure wore a long white nightgown, the low-cut V of its neckline revealing a large, oddly shaped knife jutting out of her upper chest. There was no blood, though. The figure looked weirdly virginal, like a sacrifice.

Long blond hair framed her vacant, beautiful face, a black ribbon fastened around her throat. Her head was cocked off to one side, almost resting on her shoulder.

Then the spotlight went out, the car took a hard right, and we burst through another set of double doors into the night air.

As we stumbled away from the haunted house, and as I cast glances back at the cloaked operator, Debbie took my arm and laughed. "Look at you, Tom!" she teased me. "You look even more shaken up than I am!"

***

After that year, the speedway shut down and stores began to sprout up from its lot.

I married young. Not Debbie, but an attractive young woman named Paula I met at the University of Lowell. We divorced young, too.

Between wives at twenty-four – the year being 1981 – and feeling rather lonely as Christmas neared, I decided to accept my cousin Bill's invitation to spend the holiday with his family. Following his own career move, Bill had settled way up in Ellsworth, Maine.

Maybe not the best time to take a long drive to Maine, though. Snow was beginning to fall across an already snowy landscape, the sky weighing heavily above me like a ceiling of solid white stone. I kept myself cozy, though, with frequent stops for hot coffee and an endless stream of Christmas music on the radio.

Radio stations would fade in and out, however, as I passed across the New England states, and maybe...maybe...this accounted for what occurred when my car entered a terrain of forested hills – misty through the falling snow – and wide open hollows. I crested one gradual rise to find a long, low dip in the land spread before me. Nat King Cole was drowned out in a sudden wash of static. And through the crackling disruption, distantly, I heard other music. It was very faint, but it almost sounded like the music of a calliope.

And it was as my car started descending into that broad lowland that I spotted the double Ferris wheel, looming above a fringe of evergreens on the horizon.

The bulbs that bejeweled the Ferris wheel glowed through the mist, and even from here I could tell the wheels were turning against the sky, like a machine wringing the snow from the air.

A carnival...in winter? Up here in a lonely space between small, far-flung Maine towns?

And...could it be that one? But surely there was more than one carnival that featured a double Ferris wheel.

Despite the heat turned high in my car, I shivered. I had the uncanny feeling that, unconsciously, I had been following the carnival across the land. Across the years.

Even more uncanny was the feeling that maybe the carnival was following me.

The road snaked between hills, through long corridors of trees. When I ascended a rise on the opposite side of the wide basin, I expected to have a better view of the Ferris wheel, and probably more of the carnival.

Instead, I had lost sight of it altogether.

I was tempted to turn off, to turn back, and try to find it again. Find the right path to reach it. But for what? Why?

The snow was beginning to pick up, threatening a real blizzard, and afternoon was wearing on. I knew I couldn't afford any such detour.

The calliope music had faded, and so did the static a few moments later, Gene Autry taking its place.

On my drive back home to Massachusetts, a few days later, I watched for the carnival to reappear.

It did not.

***

I am fifty-two now. I remarried at twenty-six, found happiness with a woman who maybe wasn't any goddess, but who loved me and gave me a daughter – who has in turn given me a grandson. Maybe we weren't so happy that our then nineteen-year-old daughter gave us this grandson so early, but I can't complain about my best buddy in the world.

Gerry is a precocious first grader, better on the computer than I am. He loves video games, too, scary ones that make me start and flinch to watch. Movie monster toy figures, all that cool boy stuff. Maybe he's a little morbid, but it may be the times.

I took my best buddy out with me on the flimsiest of excuses, everywhere on my errands. This evening I was bringing him back to my daughter's apartment in my old hometown of Eastborough – though my wife and I still lived in Worcester, ourselves – sharing between us the last of an order of large fries from our stop for some burgers, when from the corner of my eye I saw something like a constellation in the shape of a giant hourglass, glowing against the slate gray November sky. When I looked over that way directly, my heart launched itself against the inside of my sternum as if our car had crashed into a wall.

It was a double Ferris wheel, towering above the intervening buildings and trees.

"Gerry," I said, without looking over at him, "want to go to the carnival?"

"Huh?" He sat up higher in his seat beside me. "What carnival?" But then he spotted it, too. "Oh wow! Yeah! But...won't Mom be mad if we don't come home now? Maybe we should call her."

"I'm sure she'll understand," I muttered, already turning my car onto another street, to take me toward that galaxy of lights slowly rotating against the sky.

Gerry didn't protest again; I was the adult and the onus was on me. I could have called my daughter, and in all likelihood would have gotten her blessing, but I didn't want to chance it lest she say no. And I didn't want to wait until tomorrow. It might not be here tomorrow.

As I followed the Ferris wheel lights, like a beacon, I was confused as to where precisely the carnival could be. Somewhere not too far from the center of Eastborough, yet I couldn't think of a space in this built-up little town that might accommodate it. But shortly before I reached that space I had figured it out. The carnival had been erected on the former site of a company called Odyllic – former because a few years ago, the whole complex of factory structures, warehouses and offices had been swept by a fire of suspicious, or at least unknown, origin. I remembered there had been concerns about toxic materials remaining after the fire – though I couldn't recall ever learning just what exactly they had produced or manufactured at Odyllic – but the buildings had all been torn down by now. As far as I knew the property had not yet found a buyer, despite the prime location right here off the ever-growing town's center.

We parked on an adjoining street, and walked with the throngs that approached the carnival, mesmerized as we were by the lights, the smells, the sounds. One of these sounds, in the background, was calliope music...and I shuddered.

I bought a block of tickets from a gray-faced old woman with one white, blind eye seated in a booth that reeked of her body odor, and then Gerry was bolting to join the queue in front of a ride that made me nauseous just watching its insane spinning and gyrations. Its operator, a burly young man with a shaved head and spirals tattooed all over his face like a Maori warrior, saw me watching him and ran his tongue over his lips. I looked away quickly.

So was this the same carnival, then? I couldn't be sure. Some features, like the Ferris wheel, the merry-go-round, looked all too familiar, but there were so many newer rides and attractions, updated trailers from which food was sold or out of which games were played. Gerry survived his dizzying ride, though he wove like a drunken man as he walked toward me – grinning drunkenly, too. We continued exploring, Gerry somehow finding room in his little belly for all manner of junk food despite our recent fast food excursion. More and more I suspected this was indeed the same carnival I remembered...transfigured, mutated by the years, but the same under its patched and repainted surface. Perhaps in the interest of political correctness, but more likely due to stricter laws, I found no beer garden or girly shows.

I did find a number of sideshow tents, however, some so distinctive, so familiar that I no longer held any doubts. But there was one such tent that I didn't recall ever having encountered before in all the years I had attended. The main sign outside read: HEADLESS WOMAN – *STILL ALIVE!* Another sign showed a woman with a clean, bloodless stump for a neck, dressed in a long white gown and seated on a chair. Above this, the words: SEE HER LIVING BODY – WITHOUT A HEAD!

"Cool!" Gerry exclaimed, now having noticed the signs, too. We drew closer, near enough to read a placard that purported to give the woman's story. It was in the form of a newspaper article, even including a blown-up photo of a car wreck, supposedly dated June, 1981. It read:

"PROM QUEEN DECAPITATED IN FREAK CAR ACCIDENT.

ELLSWORTH, MAINE. On her ride home from Ellsworth High School's prom last night, prom queen Mary DeAngelo was involved in a tragic accident when the car she was riding in rear-ended a tractor trailer truck that had come to an unexpected stop. The driver, Mary's eighteen-year-old boyfriend John Harlequin, was killed instantly, but Mary's body was rushed to Maine Coast Memorial Hospital, where in a revolutionary procedure doctors managed to maintain Mary's vital processes...even after having to remove her ruined and mostly severed head. Though her headless body continues being sustained by a variety of experimental life support systems, doctors admit they can offer little more for her than a form of living death."

Gerry read the whole story, and repeated, "Cool!" He looked up at me, tugging my hand. "Let's check it out, Grampy!"

I stared at the crude painting of the woman seated in her chair, shapely and weirdly alluring despite her ghastly state, then tried to look into the tent itself, but of course my view was impeded by a canvas partition and the line of bodies streaming in to have a look. I said, "I've heard of this kind of thing, Gerry...it's just a rip-off. It's a trick they do with mirrors."

"Maybe, maybe not. You see the story, Grampy? Experimental stuff! Come on, come on!" More tugging at my hand.

I turned to the man collecting money for the attraction, handed over the fee and got in line. It wasn't until we were at the mouth of the tent that for some odd, niggling reason I glanced back at the man. Though elderly, he appeared to have once been in good physical condition. Except for a fringe of white hair, he was bald, a cigarette hanging from his lips.

"Come on, Grampy!" Gerry pulled at me, made me realize I was lagging at the entrance though it was our turn to enter. I tore my gaze from the old man, and entered the tent.

And there, across the room, she sat...the Headless Woman. As in the painting, she sat up straight in a wooden chair, her hands folded in her lap, wearing a long white gown. A barrier of velvet ropes held back the rubes who filed slowly past her, as if past Lenin or Ho Chi Minh in their glass cases, giggling and making witty wisecracks the woman would have heard a million times, if she'd had ears.

"Wow," Gerry whispered, pressing against my leg as we edged closer to her in the line.

Over a crackling intercom, a warbling recorded voice (was this the voice of the old man outside?) kept up an ongoing spiel. Most of it reiterated what was presented in the phony newspaper article outside, but there was also this: *"She is not a mannequin. She is not a dummy. She is alive...the devices that circulate her vital fluids also preserving her youthful body, while her head has long since vanished from this earth..."*

Not a mannequin. I thought of a long ago year that I had visited this carnival...the haunted house ride...

Eight tubes, like tentacles, sprouted up from the center of the woman's neck stump, supported by the arms of an apparatus like that from which an IV bag would hang, before most of them snaked down into a contraption resting beside her chair, covered in gauges, toggles and glowing red lights. One tube connected with a tank of oxygen, though, while two others ran into bottles of bubbling fluid set atop the contraption, one containing a yellowish fluid and the other fluid dark red. There was an electronic humming sound, a gurgling of the liquids circulating through those two bottles, and another sound that — as I got closer — I realized was a subdued wheezing.

As my eyes took her in — her young woman's curves evident through that shroud-like gown with its low V neckline — I saw the woman's primly folded hands suddenly twitch and flutter for several seconds before they settled down again.

"Shit!" Gerry hissed.

"Gerry," I scolded him distractedly. We were directly opposite the woman now, but people were pressing behind us, urging us not to linger too long.

Even still, it was long enough for me to notice the vertical white scar in the hollow above the woman's collarbones.

"It's real, isn't it, Grampy?"

I stepped out of the line. Right up to the velvet ropes that were all that separated the girl and myself. I leaned my body across the ropes, reached out and took hold of the woman's left hand.

"Hey, man," said someone behind me, "you shouldn't be doing that."

I squeezed her hand. And after a moment, it squeezed back. The hand was warm, alive. Like the sign outside advertised...STILL ALIVE.

"Grampy, come on!" Gerry pulled at my other hand. "Come on, before you get in trouble!"

I allowed him to pull me away. The girl's small hand slipped out of mine. I saw it fold across her right hand again, resting on her thighs.

I glanced back at her one last time as Gerry and I moved toward the tent's exit.

"Hey, don't cry, Grampy," my grandson told me gently. "I'm sure she doesn't feel anything."

"I hope not, Gerry," I said. "I hope not."

Under a now black and crystalline sky, we walked away from the sideshow tent, and I threw a look back at the silent old man, oblivious to me as he accepted more money, more offerings for his debased goddess. Was she under his spell...or, in a way, might he be under hers?

"Come on," I said, "let's get home before your mom gets too worried."

We walked back to our car against the flow of more curious, bewildered people finding their way to the unannounced carnival.

The Ferris wheel receded in my rearview mirror.

The carnival was gone the next day.

And it hasn't returned to Eastborough since.

WALTERED STATES

After several evenings of sitting on the carpet with me so we might watch TV together, my new neighbor Hee – achingly adorable little Hee – suggested we both sit in my recliner instead. We were pressed into it so snugly that she was practically in my lap. I was afraid that she would take note of my subsequent state of tumidity, but if she did she didn't call attention to it. She watched TV with a zealot's devotion. Changing the channel with my remote, she suddenly exclaimed, "*Oh, oh,* I've been wanting to watch this documentary about Rake and Widget!" She set the remote down on a smooth brown thigh (oh lucky, lucky remote) and clapped her hands like a child half her age (she had told me she was eighteen, which was a relief – her personality had led me to think she was a year or two younger).

"Who are Rake and Widget?"

"A music group. This is one of those new channels I've been watching."

I asked, "Where do you think these new channels are coming from?"

"Other dimensions," she said easily. "I sure wish Rake and Widget were in this dimension – I love them. Shh, now." She pressed a finger to my lips, and I had an impulse to take it wholly into my mouth but she drew it away first.

The documentary began by following a musical performer of this other dimension named Walter Egan, as a limousine delivered him at some TV or movie studio, a handheld camera shadowing him all the way. This Walter Egan had an attractive head of fluffy, snowy hair and looked unpretentiously casual in his dark glasses, black t-shirt and jeans. Inside the studio, on a small sound-stage around which were gathered cameras and clusters of lights, a flurry of smiling, more self-consciously attired individuals greeted the musician enthusiastically. Chief among these grinning hand-shakers was a slender youngish man who introduced himself to Egan as Teddy Winsome, his tan set off by his expensive light-colored shirt and slacks.

"Walter," Teddy Winsome gushed, pumping Egan's hand, "I can't tell you how exciting it is that you could make it today to watch Rake and Widget shoot this video."

"Well, it was fun to be flown in here for this," said Egan. "I'm flattered these guys wanted to cover my song."

"Oh, they love *Tunnel O' Love*. It's such a cool song, Walter; it has to be the raunchiest song I've ever heard. I think that's why the boys thought it would be fun to do it. It was very important to them that you get to see the shoot. God, we're all such fans of your work, here!" He waved an arm to encompass the large, scattered crew of technicians, camera operators, makeup artists, publicity people and the like. Winsome went on, "I've been meaning to check out some of your newer work, like *Walternative* – what a great title that is! But *Magnet and Steel* from '78 – oh wow, Walter, who doesn't love that song? Such a classic. I had such a crush on Stevie Nicks when I was a teenager – and who didn't, huh? I suggested to Rake and Widget they try to get her to do backing vocals for their cover of *Tunnel O' Love*, like she did for you, but ah..." his smile flickered and he shrugged "...they have their own vision, you know. They're the artists, not me, right?" Winsome gave a nervous-sounding little laugh. He had an anxious sort of energy, like a dog waiting to be swatted again with his master's rolled up newspaper.

I noticed, and it seemed to me that Egan noticed too, that there were some dark red stains on the front legs of Winsome's slacks below the knees, as if he might have spilled some food on himself or maybe knelt down in something wet, but Winsome didn't appear to notice the stains himself.

"So, ah, are you the director, Teddy?" Egan asked.

"Director? Oh no," Winsome chuckled, darting a look over his shoulder, perhaps startled by the sound of the crew behind him as they rearranged the position of a set of lights. "Rake and Widget direct themselves. I'm their liaison here."

"Liaison?"

"Their agent, more simply."

Egan nodded, glancing over at the large greenscreen backdrop the cameras and lights were trained on. The performers would be photographed against this field of lime green, and another background or series of backgrounds later added behind them using the process called chroma key. Looking back to Winsome, the singer said, "You know, sorry to say I'd never heard of these guys before."

Winsome blinked at Egan several times, his smile uncertain, as if he thought the songwriter might be kidding him. He wagged his head. "*Rake and Widget*, Walter. They're huge right now." He waved a scolding finger at Egan and joked, "You know, it's not the seventies anymore, Walter."

Egan smiled politely and said, "Well Teddy, I'm sorry, but I follow all kinds of music, and I just never heard of these guys until the request to cover my song. And I still haven't had the chance to hear anything by them. What kind of style do they have, anyway?"

"Oh, they're very versatile! They can do just about any kind of genre. Rockabilly, reggae, blues, punk..."

"Teddy! Teddy!" someone called. "It's the boys!"

Egan and Winsome turned – Winsome with a brittle grin pinned onto his face – and the handheld camera that had been bobbing beside them, covering their conversation, whipped around woozily and settled on two figures as they approached the pair.

The figures couldn't have been more different. One of them – Rake, I was to learn in a moment – was very tall and rail thin, appearing all the taller and thinner in his tight black jacket and tight black jeans. He wore black cowboy boots, and a bolo tie with a large turquoise stone offset by his black shirt. On his head, brim pulled low, was a black straw cowboy hat. It further shadowed eyes that were already deep-set in a gaunt, ashen face. His long sideburns, mustache and goatee were so black and geometrically trimmed that they looked like barely convincing theatrical appliances.

The documentary cut to a close-up of Egan, his eyes unreadable behind their dark lenses but his mouth hanging open a little, as he took in the smaller — much smaller — of the musical duo.

Widget had a waddling, floating sort of walk, his feet rising too high in an exaggerated simulation of walking. He was maybe thirty-five or forty inches tall, with the proportions of a child or dwarf, his stubby arms floating out to his sides. He wore a white, short-sleeved dress shirt under a green set of lederhosen with traditional suspenders and drop front flap. His glossy hair looked like a dollop of blood red ice cream atop his head, his bunched cheeks freckled and huge eyes emerald green. His jaw was hinged, and his limbs jointed, because Widget was a doll who moved as if suspended from wires — though I saw no wires, from where I sat. I even saw Egan look up at the ceiling of the sound-stage, as if he might find some puppeteers dressed in black hiding up in the rafters, but from the way he jerked his head this way, then that, and looked down again at Widget in incredulity, I assumed that he spotted no such puppeteers.

Rake continued forward until he stood beside, loomed over, the two men, but Widget had lagged behind, distracted by a pretty female crew member whose wrist he had taken in his articulated little fingers. When the camera turned his way again, Widget was heard saying to the woman in a lilting, high-pitched voice, "Oh come on, baby — once you go mannequin you'll never go man again."

"Widget," Winsome called, "I want you to meet Walter Egan. Rake, meet Walter."

"Sure is a pleasure, mm-hm," the tall, black-clad figure drawled in a deep monotone, shaking Egan's hand. Did the rock singer actually flinch at his grip? Was it that strong? Or that cold?

"Nice to meet you guys, too," Egan said, squeezing circulation or warmth back into his right hand with his left.

At last Widget came walking over. It almost appeared that his feet didn't always touch the ground as he moved. "Yeah, hi, Walter. So let's get this road on the show, already. Where are those backup whores?" His head twisted 360 degrees, apparently in search of some women who would appear in the video, too.

Winsome said, "Widget, I was telling Walter that I had suggested getting his friend Stevie Nicks to do backing vocals for the song."

"Fuck that," Widget chirped, his voice sweeter than the sugared tears of angels. "But I wouldn't mind slipping her my Louisville Slugger."

Rake concurred, "She's a fine lookin' little filly, I'll give you that, mm-hm."

Widget said, "I did give her a very special invitation to come down and watch us shoot the video, too, but she turned me down." One of his eyes winked at Egan with a wooden click.

Egan just stared back at the doll for a few beats, his mouth leaning toward a scowl, but then he tried on a belated smile in an obvious attempt to keep things pleasant, and said, "Well, um, since I'm here maybe it would be fun for the video version if, I don't know, I did some backing vocals for the chorus with the backup girls, or something."

"A cameo!" Winsome said brightly, turning to Widget with a grin that seemed to quiver with pure dread.

Widget said in that angelic voice of his, "We're Rake and Widget, not a fucking trio. Look, we just want to use your song – this isn't like a fucking Walter Egan tribute album or anything."

"Now, Widget," Winsome said, wagging a gently scolding finger.

The puppet turned to Winsome and gave him an abrupt kick in the right shin, with a crack of wood against bone. The cause of the dark stains on the man's pants suddenly became apparent. Winsome clenched his teeth and doubled over a little, but straightened up quickly, smiling again, his eyes tearing.

"Now *what?*" the puppet demanded of Winsome. His articulated eyebrows had turned down over his eyes in a look of cherubic fury.

"Hey, hey, come on now!" Egan said, taking a step forward as if to put himself between Winsome and the diminutive marionette, should Widget move to kick the man again. "What's the problem here? You're way out of line."

"*I'm* out of line?" Widget said.

"Wait, wait, wait. Hold on, boys." It was Winsome who stepped between Egan and Widget, chuckling as he said, "Let's not get silly, here." He took the rock singer's arm and pulled him over to the side, out of earshot. In a hurried whisper teetering at the edge of panic, Winsome said, "Walter...*please*, now. Just hang in there, okay? Rake and Widget are visiting here from...somewhere else, and we just want to keep them happy." His hand closed tightly on Egan's wrist, and his tone became even more desperate. "We don't want to make them angry!"

"Well I'm starting to get a little angry, here, myself, Teddy. Look at the way that thing kicked you, man!"

"*Shhhhh!*" Winsome's eyes bulged. "I'm okay, it doesn't matter, just...play along please, will you? Look, I'm going to write you a check before you leave, for the use of your song and for...just being cool. It'll be a very generous check, Walter. Just...stay cool."

"Yeah, well, whatever. But you're the one with the bloody shins, Teddy."

"That a boy, Walter. Let's get back in there and have some fun." With his hand on Egan's back, Winsome began steering the singer to rejoin the others, but Egan stopped and turned to the liaison again.

"Teddy...so is it Rake who controls Widget?"

Winsome looked utterly confused, as though he'd been addressed in a foreign language. "Controls?"

"I mean, who does his voice?"

Winsome laughed, as if Egan were pulling his leg. "Nobody does his voice, Walter. He does his own voice. This is Rake and Widget, not Milli Vanilli."

Walter and Winsome stood off to one side as an opening shot for the video got underway. It wasn't at first apparent what would appear behind Rake and Widget, later, in place of the greenscreen.

Here, between bits of the video shoot, shown from different angles, sections of the finished video were cut into the documentary. The background turned out to be a brightly-lit, tiled tunnel like one might find leading into a subway station, its ceiling arched, its walls and ceiling and even the floor painted glossy pink. All of it dripping wet, streams of moisture running down the wall tiles to join puddles on the floor.

Against this background, Rake and Widget appeared to be constantly walking toward the camera, as if through an endless tunnel. In reality, Rake and Widget were walking on a slowly moving treadmill on the sound-stage, Rake's long legs working in easy strides, his upper body rigid, while Widget had assumed a kind of stomping rhythm that matched the song's raunchy beat, his body moving side-to-side, his fists looking balled at his sides for trouble, his brows lowered in an expression apparently meant this time to look intense instead of furious. Had his hard wooden jaw been replaced at some point? His former sweetly smiling mouth was now more of a naughty pout.

First, Rake began singing. The deep monotone of his singing voice was little different from his speaking voice. His style was a little bit country, a little bit sepulchral. And his eyes never blinked.

Rake sang:

"Anytime you want me to do a little chore

Don't you know I'm waiting down at your back door

Indicate the feeling that you think is fine

And you know your wish would soon be mine"

Now Widget took the chorus. In his seraphic, singsong singing voice, he tended to draw out certain words, making his voice even cuter. He sang:

"Tunnel of love, tunnel of love

Ooh, baby, take me for a ride

Tunnel of love, tunnel of love

Ooh, mama, take me inside"

"Inside" being delivered by Widget as, "Iiiiinsiiiiide."

Now back to Rake, who sang:

"Ooh, you're such a comfort, ooh, you're such a thrill

Ooh, the way you hold me when you say you will"

And Widget took up:

"I'm like a volcano ready to erupt

Baby, when you treat me to your sweet, sweet stuff"

He stretched out this last as, "Sweeeeet, sweeeeet stuff."

The camera cut to Egan's face as he watched the shoot. The musician was shaking his head. Then an angle on Widget again, still stamping his feet as he marched, his intense expression making him resemble a baby trying to pass gas. He sang:

"Tunnel of love, tunnel of love

Ooh, baby, take me for a ride

Tunnel of love, tunnel of love

Ooh, mama, take me inside"

The chorus was also picked up this time by the backup singers, three attractive women – one white, one black, one Oriental – in skintight red rubber jumpsuits, who came crawling out of a sewer grate in the set's floor. In the finished video, they writhed and contorted sensuously behind Rake and Widget, seemingly following them through that endless pink tunnel. Then, it was Rake's turn again:

"Dancing down the street to the tune in my head

Thinking of the nights spent in your warm bed

I'm anticipating, watching time go by"

And Widget delivered the line:

"It's so stimulating between your thighs"

He sang it as, "Betweeeeen your thighs." Then, his jaw opened and a hinged wooden tongue waggled out. He and the backup girls sang:

"Tunnel of love, tunnel of love

Ooh, baby, take me for a ride

Tunnel of love, tunnel of love

Ooh, mama, take me inside

Take me inside"

Somewhere above, something let go — buckets tipped or balloons were burst — and a cascade of water came crashing down on the backup singers, who turned their faces up to catch the sudden downpour. While they rubbed their hands over their wet chests and bellies, Rake droned:.

"Tunnel of love, tunnel of love

Ooh, baby, take me for a ride

Tunnel of love, tunnel of love

Pretty little filly, take me for a ride"

It would gradually become obvious, through the course of the documentary, that Rake managed to slip "pretty little filly" or "silly little filly" into every song they covered. Widget took over:

"Tunnel of love, tunnel of love

Ooh, baby, take me for a ride

Tunnel of love, tunnel of love

Ooh, mama, take me inside"

Camera on Egan again. He had turned his back and was walking away, still shaking his head. Noticing this, Winsome darted anxiously after him, trying to catch his arm. Against the diminished volume of the music, Winsome hissed, "Walter, please, please don't go!"

Egan stopped and thrust a thumb in the direction of the shoot. "You know, Teddy, I think they just invited me here out of pure sadism, to make me suffer what they're doing to my song."

"Come on...it's just a fun song, Walter, you know that."

"I tried to look past that 'Walter Egan tribute album' crack, but this is all just too much."

"Walter, please, please...you can't do this to me!"

"Tunnel of love, tunnel of love," Rake sang laconically,

"Ooh, filly, take me for a ride

Tunnel of love, tunnel of love

Ooh, mama, ooh, mama

Tunnel of love, tunnel of love

Ooh..."

Widget had finally noticed Egan's departure, and screeched, "Hey! What the problem over there, Teddy?"

The music was cut off abruptly. The crew froze in place like a herd of deer caught in headlights. The backup trio quit their gyrations and stood dripping. Winsome whirled around, teetered as if he might faint, but caught himself and stammered, "Ahh...sorry to distract you, Widget. We were just talking about the song."

"What *about* the song?" the rosy-cheeked puppet demanded.

"Um...well, I was saying how Bruce Springsteen has a song called *Tunnel of Love*, too, but that Walter's song came out ten years earlier, and, ah..."

Widget snorted. "Ooh, wow, what an innovator. Did he invent the Internet, too?"

"That's it, man, that's it," Egan said to Winsome. He took a step back in the direction of the stage and called to Widget, "What is it with you? Supposedly you like my song, and you treat me like this?"

"Fuck your song, then," Widget said. "We'll scrap it from the album and do a cover of Springsteen's song instead. Right, Rake?"

"Yep, little feller. Do the Boss instead, mm-hm."

"Hey, go for it, Sling Blade," Egan said.

"Ah, get the fuck out of here!" Widget called back sweetly.

"Shut up, you freakin' ventriloquist's dummy."

"You fucking idiot," Widget retorted. "Clearly I'm a marionette!"

"Okay, Walter, come on," Winsome said, pulling him away toward the door. "You're going to have to leave, I'm sorry...you've stirred them up enough. God, now there's going to be hell to pay!"

"Well good luck to you with that, Teddy," Egan told him. And over his shoulder he shouted to Widget, "Hey, keep wishing on a star and maybe someday you'll be a real boy, Pinocchio!"

"Fuuuuuck youuuuu, Egan!" the marionette shrieked.

The scene cut after this, and led into another segment that was really much the same thing. A singer named Bruce

Springsteen was invited to watch Rake and Widget shoot a video for their cover of his song *Tunnel of Love*. Like Walter Egan, this performer also appeared not to have heard of the duo before despite Winsome's assurances that they were "massive" with the young crowd right now. The same set was employed, the treadmill in front of a greenscreen (the same background, added later, of a pink-painted tunnel), the same cavorting rubber-sheathed backup singers. But Springsteen, plainly appalled, put a stop to the proceedings quickly. Widget hurled some abuse, and Winsome took the rock star aside to try to calm him down. "Bruce, come on – it's *Rake and Widget*, man!"

"Okay, then!" Widget yelled. "If you don't like that one, let's try another one of your songs!" Stomping in place with his lowered brows and wooden pout, the puppet launched into a rollicking number called *On the Dark Side*.

"That isn't my song!" Springsteen barked. "That's John Cafferty and the Beaver Brown Band!"

Widget stopped singing and said, "What are you talking about – of course that's one of your songs!"

"It isn't my damn song! I think I'd know!"

"Okay, right, whatever you say. How about this one, then?" And the marionette launched into a rollicking number called *The Boys are Back in Town*.

"That isn't my song either and you know it!" Springsteen bellowed, causing Widget to cut his singing. "It's Thin fucking Lizzy!"

"Ah, get the fuck out of here, you washed up has-been!" the puppet raged. Springsteen started toward him but Winsome struggled to hold him back. Widget added, "And if you ever disrespect me again, I'll shove my cock so far down your throat you'll be coughing up splinters for a week!"

After this, an excerpt was shown of a video the duo had managed to complete: their cover of a song called *Little Green Bag* by the George Baker Selection (who made no appearance in the documentary). The video started with Rake's long, thin, black-clad legs walking into the frame in slow motion, followed by Widget's stumpy limbs also wearing black trousers, his floating feet barely lighting on the ground as usual. The camera setup changed to a long shot to show that Widget wore a miniature dress suit like a child might wear to its baptism. Both he and Rake wore dark glasses. Later in the video Widget was shown dancing wildly in this attire, his toddler's legs blurring in a frenzied jig, pouting and drawing forked fingers past his eyes.

The documentary took an interesting turn in another direction, interviewing the three backup singers seen in the *Tunnel O' Love/Tunnel of Love* videos. The black girl complained about Widget's advances ("One time I felt something poking me in the butt and I turned around and that little fucker was smiling up at me. It was his goddamn nose."). But more intriguing was a story the white girl had to share, sniffling and dabbing at tears while the Oriental girl put an arm around her shoulders consolingly. This young woman related:

"One time I was looking for Rake and Widget to ask them something about the next day's shoot – they were the directors, ya know? – and I knocked on their trailer's door. I didn't hear anything, so I opened the door and called out for them. I saw a blue kind of light, like TV light, in another room, so I went inside the trailer and followed it. And I saw...oh God..."

"What did you see?" asked an off-screen interviewer.

"Widget was in the corner of their little kitchen, sitting on the floor and kind of slumped down with his head hanging to the side, like this." She demonstrated. "His eyes were open, but he wasn't moving. In this funny blue light, I saw that he had strings. Strings, like a puppet!"

"You mean like a marionette?"

"Right, like that. I'd never seen them before, but they showed up in this light for some reason, kind of shiny and glowing. But they, they looked like they went straight up through the trailer's ceiling!"

"And what was this funny blue light?"

"It came from a big glass jar on the kitchen table. Something was inside it, floating in water or whatever and glowing blue. It looked like...maybe like a head of cabbage, or some cauliflower."

"And you saw Rake, too?"

"Yes," she choked. "Rake was sitting on a chair in front of this little table, kind of slumped forward, too, with his head drooping down like he was drunk. His eyes were open, but they were rolled up all white. His...his cowboy hat was on the table, and...oh God...and I swear, the top of his head was *open*. Like someone had sawed the top of his skull off! And it was just black inside...all black inside his head!"

PATRONS OF THE DARK ARTS

Nothing was provided after this segment, by the interviewer or a narrator, to explain the significance of the woman's disclosure, to elaborate on it or pursue it in any way. Instead, following this it was another scene wherein a performer was called in to watch Rake and Widget interpret one of his songs in a video. This artist was what was called a "rapper," with the stage name Ice E (his full stage name being Ice E. Conditions, formerly Ice Dover). This man looked wary and ready for hostility right from the start, once he'd had his first look at the singing duo who had invited him. Rake was dressed as usual, but Widget wore a baseball cap fitted on his head sideways, a shiny sports jacket and matching pants, baggy and riding low, and a series of gaudy gold chains. But if Ice E was wary before, he was clearly fuming once the shooting got underway. Rake and Widget took turns signing his song *King of Humility*, the puppet starting off with:

> *"The other day I drove my 'cedes back to my old hood*
>
> *All the folks there thought I was gone for good*
>
> *Told them as I stepped out from behind the wheel*
>
> *Even with all my fame I was keeping it real"*

Then Rake, stiff as a board while Widget stomped in place beside him and gestured toward his own chest with his little arms, sang without a drop of inflection:

> *"My mansion's got a wine cellar full of champagne*
>
> *When they stocked it up they had to use a crane*
>
> *But now I stood on the corner with all my old crew*
>
> *Tossing back a forty of our favorite old brew"*

And Widget again, with his surly lowered brows and wooden pout:

"I'm fuckin' all the bitches

While you just masturbate

I'm buried in riches

But my head is on straight

I'm the king of humility

Can't you see?

Ain't no motherfucker more humble than me!"

Of course, the last bit was sung liltingly as: "...more huuuuumble than me."

"Hold up, hold up," Ice E roared, moving forward into the stage lights and waving his arms, "what the fuck is this shit?"

Widget waddled to the edge of the little stage they were being filmed on. "Excuse me?"

Ice E whirled and shouted at Winsome, while pointing back at Widget. "Nobody told me this freaky little midget was gonna cover my damn song!"

"Oh my God," Winsome cried, "Mr. E...please don't!"

"I ain't letting it happen! You hear me? This is bullshit!"

"Hey, 'G,'" Widget said, "we're covering your 'damn song' whether you like it or not."

Ice E turned around again, very slowly, to face the hip hop-attired puppet – his eyes bulging, white all around their pupils. "What the fuck did you say?"

Widget started weaving his head from side-to-side, as he repeated, "I said, we're going to cover this song...and if you don't like it you can kiss my wooooooden ass –" he tilted his head to one side, batted his eyes adorably and added in his sweeter-than-sweet voice "– *bitch*."

Winsome and one of the crew members managed to restrain the rapper for a moment, but he tore free, reached inside his jacket and pulled out a semi-automatic pistol. He thrust his arm out to its full length, the pistol held horizontally rather than vertically, and fired off shot after cracking shot.

("Oh my God! Oh my God!" Hee cried out, so tightly wedged in my recliner beside me, "I didn't hear this happened!")

Widget was thrown back, the baseball cap falling from his head. Rake went down on a knee beside his sprawled partner, while Ice E spun around and bolted for the exit. People were screaming, pulling out cell phones to call for the authorities, or to take videos of the fallen celebrity. Winsome dropped to both knees, holding his head between his hands, squeezing his eyes shut and presumably mouthing a prayer.

The documentary camera rushed closer to shoot over Rake's shoulder, and there lay Widget, struck by multiple bullets. Vivid red blood was leaking from the holes punched in the puppet, forming a growing puddle under him in which splinters floated. Rake held one of his chubby little articulated hands, and looking up at him with half-closed lids, Widget said, "Aw, fuck, man, I'm dying."

"Hold old, little feller," Rake said tonelessly.

"I'm fucking dying, man."

"I'm with you, little feller, mm-hm."

A sound between a dry rattle and a wet gurgle was emitted, and then Widget's wooden tongue was thrust from between his painted teeth.

If that didn't make the outcome clear enough, the next sequence left no room for doubt. Expensive cars and limousines were driving up in front of a funeral parlor. Camera crews and journalists from TV stations and newspapers crowded about for shots of the celebrities who emerged from the cars and moved inside for the ceremony.

The documentary switched to the proceedings inside – and there among the milling VIPs was the singer Walter Egan, dressed in a nice suit and tie, but with an electric guitar slung across his body. Teddy Winsome stood beside him, and was saying, "Please just do this, Walter. I'll have a nice check for you after it's all over, believe me."

The musician sighed, and said, "That's fine, thanks – not that I'm as mercenary as you think, Teddy."

The camera cut to Rake standing over his partner's coffin, which more resembled a shoe box. Inside, dressed in his trademark short-sleeved white shirt and green lederhosen, the rosy-cheeked, baby-faced puppet smiled blissfully. Rake removed his black cowboy hat and held it over his chest. When he did so, he inadvertently exposed a white scar that entirely encircled the top of his head, set off by his slicked black hair.

"Goodbye, little feller," he said, "mm-hm."

Then, a cut to Walter Egan playing his electric guitar, which he'd plugged into an amplifier, accompanying Rake as the latter sang for the assembled mourners:

"Amazing Grace, how sweet the sound,

That saved a wretch like me....

I once was lost but now am found,

My pretty little filly."

After the ceremony, when the attendees were once again forming little groups to talk, Winsome thanked Egan and handed him his check. "Thanks," the singer said, folding it away. "So, ah, whose request was it that I play, anyway? Rake?"

"No, no." Winsome pointed across the room. "It was their request."

Egan turned to look, as did the eavesdropping documentary camera.

There stood two very different figures. One was a female dressed in a black leotard that included a tight hood around her head, baring only her face, which was made up in white and black mime makeup. Hanging from her midsection was the upper body of a partly developed conjoined twin, the woman's leotard having been artfully extended to encompass its body, too. The parasitic twin's slack, drooling face was also made up in mime makeup, its gnarled hands convulsively thumping at some imaginary window. Beside the woman, a German Shepherd sat patiently. It wore a brass deep sea diving helmet, with the front hatch open to allow its snout to poke out.

Teddy Winsome explained brightly, "They're my new clients, Walter, and they really love your work!"

THE AFTERLIFE OF
JACOB B. COPPINS

Jacob's parents, Andrew and Hannah Coppins, learned of his death when they found taped to his door an obituary he himself had created on his computer. It was all quite convincingly done; so much so that his mother gasped when she first saw it, thinking without thinking that someone had somehow got into their home (well, into the space above their garage, more precisely) to leave this notice for them to discover. But she realized the truth when her husband said, "Oh no...he's done it. He said he was going to do it, and he did it." As if they had found their only child's twenty-six-year-old corpse hanging purple-faced from a rope, or with his upper head flowered open from a shotgun blast. The obituary read:

Jacob Brandon Coppins

Jacob B. Coppins, 26, of 98 Milk Street, Eastborough, MA, died of natural causes on October 6th, in his family home. A memorial service will be performed at the Pelletier Funeral Home, 4 Church Street, on October 9th from 6-8 PM.

Jacob lived all his life in Eastborough, MA, attending school there before going on to attend the Foundation Year program at the Massachusetts College of Art and Design in Boston. Jacob furthered his studies in History of Arts and Liberal Arts, in pursuit of a Bachelor of Fine Arts degree, but unfortunately was forced to abandon these plans due to his inability to secure loans and the lack of financial support from his parents.

Jacob sought to support himself as a freelance graphic designer, creating logos for local bands and businesses, such as the label for the microbrew Eastborough Oatmeal Cookie Ale, of which he was especially proud. Life's challenges took their toll, however, and Jacob succumbed to his long struggle before realizing his full potential.

Jacob is survived by his parents, Andrew and Hannah Coppins of 98 Milk Street, Eastborough, and various uncles, aunts, cousins, friends, and his former girlfriend Amy, all of whom likewise proved unable or unwilling to assist Jacob in his time of need.

In lieu of flowers, donations can be made to the Jacob B. Coppins Fund, found at www.jacobbcoppinsfund.com.

To sign Jacob's guest book, please visit:

www.pelletierfuneralhome.com.

"God damn it!" Andrew Coppins shouted when he got to the end of the obituary, which he'd been reading with moving lips. He tried rattling the knob of his son's door but it wouldn't much budge, so he then thumped the wood with the heel of his fist. "You let us in there, Jacob, right now! You hear me? Let us in!"

"Andy...Andy," his wife said, putting a hand on his arm. Though membranes of tears capped her eyes, and her voice was crumbling, she said, "we have to respect his wishes. We have to." When her husband wheeled at her with his own eyes gone large, she hastened to add, "For now. For now. Maybe he'll change his mind."

"Change his mind?"

"If he can decide to be dead, he can decide not to be dead. Let's just give him time, okay? A little time. If we push him too much, he'll just get more stubborn." She lowered her voice to a dread-filled whisper. "Maybe then do it for real."

"That would almost be better," Andrew Coppins muttered bitterly, stepping back from the door of the granny apartment over their garage they had turned over to their son upon his having left school to return home, some years back. Before then, it had been used for storage. Well, it still was, in a way. Storage for an expired son.

"What do you mean?" his wife said, incredulously.

"Nothing," Andrew groused, turning away to retreat downstairs and return to their house, adjacent to the garage. Halfway down the stairs he paused, and over his shoulder he shouted, loudly enough for someone to hear behind that locked door, "If he thinks I'm paying Pelletier for that memorial service, he's nuts!"

***

Before Jacob had left college there had been talk of giving the granny apartment to his maternal grandmother, but her poor health had required that she be interred in a nursing home. Jacob visited her there about once a month and would sit watching TV with her; old black-and-white western programs were her favorite, for some reason. She would sit up in bed eating the candies he'd brought her, and he'd see the stack of books and DVDs on the table by her bed, and he'd say to her, "Jeesh, Nana, I think you have it really good here. You don't have to work...don't have to worry about anything...you just watch movies and stuff. I'm jealous."

"Well it gets lonely, Jake," his Nana would say, always surprised by his envy. "And it's boring spending almost all my time in bed."

"Lonely? All I want to do these days is get away from people, and not get out of bed."

His Nana would sigh and say, "It's always greener on the other side."

He had a single window up here, and right now the drapes were drawn to shut out the sight of his car down there in the driveway. He'd probably lose it now; he couldn't imagine his parents taking on the payments. Oh well...he knew he could convince his mother to lend him her car when he needed it. At this point his vehicle was a doable sacrifice.

He was slouched back on his sofa – which was also his foldout bed – dressed in a MassArt t-shirt and sweatpants, with his tablet resting on one knee, but it was connected to his sizable TV and he was watching videos there. He liked to watch random videos that were suggested to him based on his subscriptions and previous searches.

After having binge-watched videos by numerous creators on the possible existence of various cryptids, over the past several days, he'd now returned his interest to the subject of mysterious structures, seemingly cell phone towers, that had reportedly appeared all over the world. According to an unorganized abundance of amateur investigators, these structures were made to look like legitimate cell phone towers used to connect up a cellular network, but they were something more or other than that. Theories about their true purpose abounded: * They had been erected by the government, or local police, to monitor the communications and hence the lives of the citizenry. * They were actually USW (ultrasonic weapons) capable of emitting crowd-controlling high-frequency blasts in case of insurrection. * They had been set up by criminals, scammers, as a way to gather credit card information and such. * They had been blended innocuously into the landscape by hostile foreign powers, perhaps to infiltrate or sabotage communications, or else they were really nuclear electromagnetic pulse weapons that could knock out power grids, sending this country into the dark ages, ultimately causing the death of millions over time.

Presently Jacob watched a video shot on a cell phone camera in Russia. Two or three young men – it was hard to tell their number; they had kept their faces off-camera – had approached one of these towers where it loomed in a bleak rural area. (So maybe it truly was Russia that had set up the towers people claimed to have singled out in this country; of course they'd want them on their own soil, to control their own people, too.) In this video, the men broke off pieces of plants and touched their stems or leaves to the base of the tower, using thick rubber gloves to protect their hands. The plants would start sizzling, and voices like radio transmissions could be heard as the plants acted as plasma speakers due to the current running into them – which caused the ions in the plants' plasma to vibrate, producing sound waves.

But as the narrator of this video explained, in English, the voice heard in these transmissions spoke in a language no one as yet could identify. Furthermore, the apparently male voice spoke much too slowly and deeply, like a vinyl record played at the wrong speed. Whatever the cause of that distortion, if it was distortion, this voice inspired a shudder in Jacob every time he saw this video.

The narrator also pointed out the foolishness of the young experimenters, who may have caused themselves serious internal injuries due to their proximity to such high voltage, though outwardly they might appear fine.

Still, Jacob had encountered even more daring, or foolish, young adventurers in other related videos. He moved on to re-watch one of these – the most amazing of those of its kind. Whoever had posted it had named this video *The Slow Gods*.

He'd read the viewers' comments on this video before. Others had said things like: "Fake!" "Photoshopped!" "Cool CGI, bro!" "Yeah, right!" For his own part, Jacob believed in the veracity of this video...believed it in his guts. His own posted comment had been: "Whoa!"

The video had been made in this country. The cell phone tower in question – one of those somehow determined to be bogus by the open-minded citizens who were investigating this matter on their own – stood at the foot of a steep grassy hill. Six young men (Jacob figured them to be between nineteen and twenty-one) stood at the base of the tower in a chain extending away from it, holding hands. A seventh person, a young woman whose voice was occasionally heard, was making the video with her phone, bursts of wind scraping past the microphone.

The last man in the chain called to her, asking if she were ready, and she replied in the affirmative. This man then called ahead to the first man in the chain and asked if he were ready.

This man, with curly black hair and a beard, wearing a black band t-shirt, seemed to hesitate before answering, but then he shouted, "Yeah...yeah, man, let's do this! Fuck it...let's do this thing!" He then took two steps forward, the whole chain shifting after him like the body of a caterpillar, and he reached up with his free hand and pressed its palm against the tower's trunk. He wasn't wearing rubber gloves.

He immediately began shrieking, his flattened hand stuck to the metal as if nailed there, and smoke started wisping around his fingers...but Jacob barely ever noticed that part. He was too busy staring at the creatures, or beings, that manifested.

There were three of them, of a kind, each as tall as a two-storey house. One was close, just behind the tower. The next stood about halfway up the hill, and the third was perched atop the hill's crest, against a backdrop of evergreen trees. They had blocky bodies like those of cattle but much larger, entirely white, with very long, very skinny stilt-like legs. The head of each was human-like: bald, with the flesh around the eyes so wrinkled that the actual eyes, if they had them, were lost in the folds. Below the nose was a thick black beard, but seemingly made of tangled shreds of rubbery flesh rather than hairs, and a similar growth of black hair-tendrils hung from the rear-end. Into the forehead of each was inscribed an X, which glowed a fluorescent purple.

If the creatures moved at all, it was too slowly to notice, and if they made any sound it was drowned out by the screams not only of the man stuck to the tower's base, but of his friends as well. To her credit, despite her own wild screaming, the woman recording the video kept on shooting, though the image did bounce around quite a bit.

The friends of the man at the front of the chain had the presence of mind to pull back on him with all their strength, perhaps as part of a pre-arranged plan. They won the tug-of-war and dislodged him, most of them tumbling into the grass atop each other like dominoes, and the three creatures blinked out of existence again. Or, that is, blinked out of perception.

"Jesus...Jesus!" the second man in the chain groaned, rolling in the grass with his scorched hands tucked into his armpits. But everyone else was rushing to the side of the man who'd been pinned in place by the high voltage coursing through his body, the woman who was recording included. When she got close to him, she cried out in horror but still kept shooting.

His right arm, swollen and shiny red, was split open deeply from wrist to elbow like a hotdog that had been microwaved too long. The interior of the wound hadn't begun bleeding yet, simply bubbled and sizzled like hot grease.

"You did it, man, you fucking did it!" one of the other men raved, helping him up into a sitting position. "Did you see that shit, dude? Did you fucking see that?"

Others crawled to him, clapped him on the back, mussed his hair, gave him quick hugs. "You are fearless, brother," one young man told him. "You *touched* it!" His words seemed to suggest that the "it" he had touched was more than just the base of the tower.

He was grinning drunkenly, proud and in a different kind of shock now.

"Do you think they're still there?" asked the young woman making the recording, as she panned her cell phone toward the empty hill. Her voice was shaky, fearful, and yet tinged with excitement. "You think they're still there...somewhere?"

***

"Ah-ha! Call the media...I've spotted a ghost!" cried Andrew Coppins.

Jacob had gotten the munchies while playing the videogame *N-Vasion*, and had thought his parents would both be asleep at this hour, but then again it was Friday. His father had caught him poking around in the refrigerator, pulling out a container of ham salad with which to make a sandwich. Jacob followed through, turned to the counter, opened the container and spooned the pink matter onto his bread.

"If you're dead," his father persisted, between gulps of the bottled water he'd come for, "why do you need to eat?"

Oh, but Jacob was ready for this argument. He smiled at his father and said, "In many cultures offerings of food are given to the dead. Egyptian priests used a spoon-thing called a pesehkaf to feed food and water to statues that represented the dead. And can you say, Halloween candy? How do you think trick-or-treating originated?"

"I remember taking you trick-or-treating," his father said. "Back when you were a small kid, instead of a big kid. Back then you told me you were going to be a veterinarian."

"Dad," Jacob turned to face him directly, "are you going to tell me you don't feel this life killing you? The *pointlessness* of it all? I'm just surprised you and Mom haven't given in yet, yourselves. That everyone everywhere hasn't given in to it."

"We'll all die someday, for real. Why rush it? Why not keep going and try to make things better?"

"*Better?* Boy, you believe all the advertisements and motivational posters and politicians, don't you? There *is* no better. This is it. *This.*" He waved around him, holding a mayonnaise-coated spoon, at nothing in particular. "The mysteries of life aren't here...they're not in your pile of bills. They're not in your tax returns. They're not in your prenup with Mom. The only real truth that's left to us is in the stuff we can't yet tell is true."

"Are you taking drugs in there? Is that it? I've been worried that I'm not smelling pot anymore...that must mean you're doing more serious stuff."

Jacob sighed. He hadn't been smoking, true, nor indulging in harder substances, though he had been buying big plastic bottles of headache-inducing cheap vodka. "Look, I'm going to finish making my sandwich. Why don't you go back to bed?"

"What if I tell my insurance company not to pay death benefits for you? Or what if I keep those benefits for myself?"

"Then, I hate to say it, Dad, but I'd be forced to sue you. I wouldn't want to, but you'd leave me no choice. You have good comprehensive insurance, very sensitive to current needs, and I thank you for that. Collecting those benefits and passing them on to me won't cost you anything more than is already deducted from your paycheck."

"You're going to have to sign forms. You and me both," Andrew said, his words going weary.

"Okay. Let me know when you get the papers."

"You might have to see a counselor first, before they pay. At least once...to clear it. You know that?"

"Yeah, I understand that. But in the end, I'm sure they will. They know how hard it is now...how young people like me feel. People are free to identify as dead if they want to. It's the ultimate freedom for a country that claims it's all about freedom."

"I guess science doesn't mean anything to you, huh? Because...shh, just between the two of us, you *know* you're really alive."

"Real freedom," Jacob told his father, slapping the top slice of bread onto his sandwich, "is the freedom from science."

"So then freedom from reality, too, huh?"

Jacob just shrugged, as if to say "so be it," as he licked the mayo off his butter knife.

***

Someone had worked up a map that pinpointed the location of all the currently known mock cell phone towers where they appeared across the United States, indicating these sites through the use of a publicly available computer program that created a three-dimensional rendering of Earth via satellite images. A short piece had been made about this map for the video-sharing website Jacob favored. What had intrigued him so much about the towers in the first place was that in this video – the first he had ever viewed on the subject, which he had chanced upon one night in the course of searching for videos that discussed conspiracies, esoteric matters, controversial mysteries, and the like – it was claimed one of the towers was situated right here in his own town of Eastborough, Massachusetts.

He'd had the 3D Earth program already installed on his PC, so he had input the longitude and latitude given in the video for the Eastborough tower, and thus had been able to zoom in on it fairly closely (though a street-level view was not available for this spot). Thus, having noted the precise location of the tower in regard to his own knowledge of his town, he had once before gone to have a look at it in person.

For the second time, he now sat in his car staring out his window at it.

The funny thing was, the enigmatic cell towers came in a variety of configurations; that is, they were not all identical in appearance and design. Some were of the type called "lattice towers," others being "guyed towers," and it was claimed a few were even massive "broadcast towers." There were none of the type known as "stealth towers," however, which could be designed to appear like a pine tree or palm tree, a tall cactus, a flagpole, or even a church steeple; Jacob imagined that would actually make them seem more suspicious, rather than nondescript. The tower in Eastborough was of the variety known as a "monopole tower," being just a two-hundred-foot pole with external antennas at its top.

This tower loomed beside an abandoned brick structure, an outer building of a former factory complex for an abrasives company...now out of business, the buildings locked up and weeds growing from cracks in the empty parking lots. Jacob had parked only a short distance from the pole, its shadow laying across his car. (It was too soon yet for his vehicle to have been repossessed.)

The Eastborough tower had a chain-link fence around it, its gate padlocked shut, as these mystery towers tended to have when they were situated in a less desolate spot. This old factory complex was, after all, just a short walk from downtown.

In one video Jacob had watched, a man who had kept his identity hidden by never allowing his face to be seen on camera had sat in his car beside one of the giant red and white broadcast towers, with microwave dishes on its flanks. This person had switched on his car radio, to the AM, and had turned the dial slowly, sifting through static until finally he found what he was looking for: a distorted-sounding transmission. An apparently male voice speaking in some kind of foreign language, this deep monotonous voice sounding much too slowed down.

Jacob turned on his own car radio, to the AM, and he too began inching his way carefully from one side of the dial toward the other. Then back again. But he discovered no mysterious broadcast.

He gave up, figured this tower simply wasn't powerful enough to enable the effect.

He ducked down in his seat a little to gaze up at the antenna array mounted at the pole's summit one last time before starting his car and driving off to get himself a coffee.

***

While seated at a corner table in a local coffee shop with his tablet in front of him, Jacob had been text messaging back and forth with a young woman he'd met on a dating site. She'd told him she was on her lunch break at work; she worked for a data storage company. He'd been attracted to the photos on her page: she had long dyed-blond hair, sharp features, a tan she showed off in photos of herself in various bikinis at various beaches, a body she displayed in form-fitting exercise outfits at the gym. She'd complimented him on his looks, too; she said she liked his beard, which was a particular point of pride with him, as it was long and full, fluffy and naturally blond. He'd asked her out and she hadn't quite accepted yet but she hadn't turned him down, either. As the end of her lunch break neared, she asked him:

"So what do you do for a living?"

"I'm not living. I identify as dead."

"Oh," she texted in reply. "Okay. So...do you get death benefits then?"

"Not yet. I'll be applying very soon. Right now I have a bit of savings." Which was true; he had $222 in the bank. He'd borrowed $200 from his mother a few days ago, before he died.

"Why'd you decide to die?"

"It's a long story, but I'd be happy to tell you over coffee."

"Look, Jake, I think you and I want very different things out of life. Oops, about 'life.' But you know what I mean. Like, if you consider yourself dead, why are you looking for someone to date?"

"Well, don't you believe in a soul? My soul still goes on. You don't just care about a person's body and what they do for a job and all, do you?"

"If you don't care about the body, only the soul, I guess that means you aren't hoping to have sex again, huh?"

"Hey, no...I mean, people's souls come closer during sex, you know."

"Listen, Jake, sorry, but I have quite a bucket list, and *dead* is at the very bottom of it. I want to find a soul mate, sure, but I'm not a necrophiliac, and I want to have children someday. I'd rather not have children that are stillborn, ya know? Like, ghost children? Ha ha." For punctuation, a laughing emoji face.

Jacob's face flushed molten, and he typed, "Intolerant fascist Barbie doll bitch." Then he quickly blocked her before she could respond.

***

For the first time, on this third instance of visiting the tower, Jacob stepped outside his car to stand in its thick band of shadow and tilt his head far back to gape up at it. It was like a great metal finger pointing at the blue, cloud-scuffed heavens.

His most recent serious relationship had been with Amy, a church-going Christian. She had told him that a hand with a finger pointing downward, portrayed on an old gravestone, represented God reaching down for the soul...while an index finger pointing up represented a hope for the soul's travel heavenward.

Heh, Jacob thought with an inward sneer. *Christianity*. No wonder they hadn't worked out (though he had read from the Bible she had gifted him with, because she was so cute).

He walked around the chain-link enclosure, across the cracked parking lot of the old abrasives factory, as if from a different angle he might spy some hidden detail that would give him *something*. Whatever something was.

And he did make a discovery. He was surprised to have done so, as if he had never entirely believed in this ill-focused conspiracy until that very moment.

Spray-painted in purple on the pavement on the far side of the tower, outside the fence, was a large X.

Jacob knelt down and laid his palm flat against the very center of the blurry-looking X. Though he felt nothing, he still smiled, because it *was* something.

***

Jacob had told his father he had taken out a loan to pay for the memorial service at Pelletier Funeral Home. ("How'd you manage a loan without a job?" Andrew had asked, but Jacob had squirmed out of the conversation.) In actuality, his mother had secretly taken an emergency loan from her retirement fund at work, which Jacob had promised to pay back to her in increments once he started receiving death benefits from his father's insurance company.

Jacob lay in a rented coffin reserved for such situations, and a small number of uncles and aunts, cousins and friends filed past, kneeling at the little bench to silently say a prayer or a few words of remembrance if they cared to. Around the viewing room on various tables were numerous photos documenting Jacob's life, in frames or taped to big sheets of cardboard. His mother, sadly resigned to his decision, had proved fairly supportive, as he had known she would, and had helped him create these photo displays and a slideshow presentation that played on her laptop, besides.

His Nana was too weak to attend, but her sister – his great aunt Ellen – attended and wept as she knelt feebly at his coffin. He wanted to open his eyes and comfort her, tell her that he only identified as dead, wasn't physically dead, but he didn't want to dismiss his own status that way. Mainly he didn't want to give her a heart attack that might result in her own funeral. Later, when he was out of the coffin, he quickly sought out her son and advised him to let Aunt Ellen know how things really were, before it was time for the actual memorial service – which he himself would be delivering to the seated guests.

When it was time for that, he stood before the now empty coffin like Christ arisen and said:

"Thank you for coming. Jacob thought highly of all of you present, whatever you might have felt about him in the past, and whatever you feel about him now.

"No one really wishes for death; they only wish for their life to be better when it's not, and they despair that a better life doesn't show on the horizon. The ultimate freedom is to choose to no longer slog toward that empty horizon..."

He searched the faces seated before him, to judge if they were impressed by these practiced words. (He saw one of his cousins looking at her phone). He had hoped to see Amy here – he'd sent her an email and two texts, none of which she'd responded to – though he wasn't surprised by her absence.

He went on: "There's a lot of hypocrisy regarding the decision Jacob made. So many, many people around the world, supposedly devoutly religious, claim that the soul lives on after death...freed from all worldly cares. But when someone chooses to continue on as dead, shedding their cloak of mortal sorrows – to go on as an unencumbered soul – too often their decision is met with disdain, or at the very least with a lack of understanding.

"It was Jacob's fondest wish that his act would help to open more eyes, and more hearts, to the decision he made...that so many other people both young and old are making in these times of unrelenting hopelessness.

"Jacob would want everyone to know that death is a liberation from the disillusionments of life. It is not the end, but the start of a new journey into the possibilities of the unknown."

Then his mother pushed a button on the funeral parlor's music system, and Nick Cave's cover of Bob Dylan's song *Death is Not the End* came over the speakers. Jacob teared up just seconds into it.

After the service people approached him to awkwardly wish him well or give their blessings, before the 8 PM closing. A coworker friend from when he'd worked at a fast food restaurant while in high school shook his hand and said, "Congratulations, man. Or, I mean —" he laughed uncomfortably "— condolences, or whatever. You know what I mean. Anyway, I envy you...I'd do the same thing myself if I had insurance that covered it."

"You can still apply for state assistance," Jacob advised him. "Slowly, more and more people are getting it. The state needs to do that — it's just too hard to go on these days, ya know?"

"Tell me about it, dude — exactly."

"They have to respect your choice, man. I'm tired of the prejudice against it."

"Sucks," his friend agreed, nodding solemnly.

***

Jacob was visiting the tower in Eastborough for the fourth time. True autumn was on the wax; leaves blew across the dead pavement like shed exoskeletons. He'd just finished having a late breakfast, alone, at the South Street Diner...a walk of less than ten minutes away. His car was still back there in the diner's lot.

While eating, he'd sent Amy another email via his tablet. She was hard to stop thinking about: a fit bleached-blond, with teeth that seemed illuminated from within. He'd felt so proud, so lucky to have her. For him she'd seemed the American Dream personified.

After sending the email, in which he told Amy how his memorial service had gone and how disappointed he'd been that she hadn't paid her respects, he saw he had an email from Greg, a friend he'd made at MassArt, who worked for a major graphic design company with offices on Union Street in Boston. Greg was excited about his imminent move to New York, where he had found an even better gig. For a moment Jacob expected Greg to go on and say that Jacob should now apply for his job, and that he'd put in a good word for him, but that part didn't come. "Fuck you, Greg," Jacob muttered, when he'd come to the end of the message.

He might still apply...*ask* Greg to recommend him. He knew, though, that with only a year completed at MassArt his credentials were bound to be inadequate. Anyway, here he was...dead. It was a decision he'd put a lot of thought into, and approached with conviction. It wasn't something one could just switch on and off, however much his parents wished that were so.

The tower reared high above him just ahead, but a short distance in front of its surrounding fence lay an odd object. As Jacob walked closer he realized it was some kind of drone, looking crab-like with its four propeller-tipped arms. He flipped it over with his shoe, saw the camera eye on its belly. There was a hole in the drone's underside, looking burnt around the edges. Had someone shot this out of the sky, on a lark?

He took several pictures of it with his phone's camera. He intended to shoot some pictures of the purple X spray-painted on the ground, too. Maybe he'd make his own video to share with others intrigued with this subject.

He glanced all around him, as if he might spy the drone's operator observing him, but saw no one lurking about. Then, he leaned back and shielded his eyes with one hand to gaze up at the tower's antenna arrays. What did those things really receive? What did they really transmit...or project?

He left the drone behind, went right up to the fence's gate and gave a little tug on the padlock. Yes, it was firmly locked. Holding on to the chain-links, he looked through them at the tower's thick, cylindrical base. Like the mast of some ancient ship discovered floating at sea, abandoned, taunting and beguiling him with its mysteries.

Jacob sighed, let go of the cage – which seemed to him like very barrier that locked him out of every success, every happiness, every reward – and circled slowly around the cell tower once, in its orbit, twice. As he completed the second orbit, something small dropped from above right at his feet. He stopped to look down at it.

It was a little brown bird with a white belly; he wasn't sure what type, as he didn't know much about such things. Thin tendrils of smoke twisted up from its dead body. He crouched down for a closer look but was afraid to touch it, lest it still be alive in actuality and jerk into sudden movement. It appeared to him that its eyes had been scorched away, and that those wisps of smoke rose from its tiny blackened sockets.

Once more, from his squatting position, Jacob looked up and up at the tower. He thought: *What is it that you don't want seen? At least...from these things that aren't ready to see it?*

***

He'd finally done it. After seemingly countless hours of game play, he'd beaten the videogame *N-Vasion*.

After blasting, slicing, and punching his way through seemingly endless hordes of the reptilian Ov-R-Lords, he'd worked his way to the Queen in her lair, twisting her bloated head from side-to-side, her vile green breath congealing in bubbles on the walls of her cavern, these bubbles quickly becoming eggs, the eggs quickly hatching into larval Ov-R-Lords. He'd dispatched her at last, and he gave a whoop as she shrieked shrilly and curled up upon herself in death.

It felt like a major accomplishment. He grinned. And his grin slowly faded as the game credits scrolled and scrolled. The proud accomplishments of strangers.

He wondered then why games always had to portray the alien, the unknown, as hostile. Why encounters with such miraculous beings were always toxic, destructive. Wasn't it possible to create a game wherein an encounter with an awe-inspiring alien entity was uplifting, transformative?

With night having fallen hours earlier, he left his granny apartment, crept downstairs and stole up to his parents' adjacent house, on the other side of a door that led into their kitchen. He put his ear close to the wood, and heard his father ranting to his mother:

"...at twenty-six-years-old! And do you know what my father was doing, when he was a *teenager?* He was killing Nazis!"

Under his breath Jacob murmured, "You're a Nazi." He turned away, despite his growling belly, and retreated back to his own little nest.

***

At least the chain-link fence had no coils or strands of barbed wire on top of it, as these fences sometimes did.

He stepped out of his car, which he'd parked a little ways down the street from the cell phone tower, in a patch of darkness between misty skirts of sodium light. It was cool outside with fall flowing in, and he looked up and down this lonely little side street, praying no police cars showed, attracted to his presence...not that he expected this. From downtown, not too far distant, he heard the occasional whisper of a passing car. It was past eleven at night.

Jacob approached the fence, his footsteps crunching lightly. As if it sought to minimize attention to itself, the tower had no light at its summit to warn low-flying aircraft, but then Jacob reminded himself it was only about two-hundred-feet tall. Thus, it stood as a silhouette against the diffused ambient glow from nearby streetlamps. He thought then that – despite their being instruments that enabled countless human beings to communicate with each other – there was little more lonesome-looking a thing than a cell phone tower.

The drone was gone, he noticed. Had neighborhood kids taken it, or someone with a more direct interest?

Curious, he looked for the dead bird. At least that was still here. He activated his phone's flashlight feature and saw that tiny black ants swarmed in its eyeholes.

Jacob had brought with him a blanket he'd kept in his car for Amy's sake; she'd always claimed to be cold, would huddle in its folds even on a summer's night, and would always thank him for it. It had felt to him like an extension of his embrace. Well, it still had a purpose. He doubled the blanket up and threw it over the top of the fence. Then, after looking up and down the street again and assuring himself the coast was as clear as it ever would be, he climbed up the rattling fence, hoisted himself over its top, and dropped to the other side.

He turned to confront the tower, for the first time with no obstacle between them.

He was shaking so violently that his teeth were on the verge of chattering. He let out a funny little laugh, and stepped a bit nearer to where the great metal trunk was rooted in the prosaic earth. An exclamation point suggesting the end of an invisible coded sentence.

"Fuck it," he said aloud. "Let's do this thing!"

Jacob closed the distance between himself and the tower, thrust both arms out in front of him, and pressed his hands flat against the metal.

The sky was jarred from black to a neon pink, marbled with violet clouds. Two nearly full moons, close by each other, one smaller than the other, took up a good section of this sky. The buildings of the shut-down abrasives factory were gone. Indeed, the cell tower was gone.

Jacob's hands were pressed against a huge dome of forehead, rumpled and furrowed. Shining into his face was purple light from a large, X-shaped wound in the colorless flesh.

The Slow God reared up, ponderously, Jacob's hands slipping away from its head. As it rose, as if in weirdly blurred slow motion, its swaying beard of black tendrils brushed against his face. Languorously, a timeless being taking all the time it wanted, it soared higher and higher against the luminous pink sky as its immensely long white legs unfolded.

As it straightened, Jacob could see – even though his eyes had boiled and bubbled away in their sockets, to make way for a new kind of sight – others of its kind behind it. A whole herd of them, facing toward him, their eyes (if they possessed them) sunken into the wrinkles of their ancient faces.

And though a human shell lay red and split and steaming in a parking lot in a town called Eastborough, in the state of Massachusetts, beside the tiny corpse of a bird, in this place Jacob raised up his arms again, his charred hands smoking like incense, and began chanting in a language he hadn't known until now, in a voice slowed down...slowed...down...to a rhythm not of alarm clock and time clock, but in synch with the patient heart-pulse of the universe, between the beats of which stretched vast gulfs of blessed nothingness.

ABOUT THE AUTHOR

Jeffrey Thomas is an American author of weird fiction, the creator of the acclaimed setting Punktown. Books in the Punktown universe include the short story collections PUNKTOWN, VOICES FROM PUNKTOWN, PUNKTOWN: SHADES OF GREY (with his brother, Scott Thomas), GHOSTS OF PUNKTOWN, and the shared world anthology TRANSMISSIONS FROM PUNKTOWN. Novels in that setting include DEADSTOCK, BLUE WAR, MONSTROCITY, HEALTH AGENT, EVERYBODY SCREAM!, and RED CELLS. Thomas's other short story collections include THE UNNAMED COUNTRY, THE ENDLESS FALL, HAUNTED WORLDS, WORSHIP THE NIGHT, THIRTEEN SPECIMENS, NOCTURNAL EMISSIONS, DOOMSDAYS, TERROR INCOGNITA, UNHOLY DIMENSIONS, AAAIIIEEE!!!, HONEY IS SWEETER THAN BLOOD, and ENCOUNTERS WITH ENOCH COFFIN (with W. H. Pugmire). His other novels include LETTERS FROM HADES, THE FALL OF HADES, BEAUTIFUL HELL, BONELAND, BEYOND THE DOOR, THOUGHT FORMS, SUBJECT 11, LOST IN DARKNESS, THE SEA OF FLESH AND ASH (with his brother, Scott Thomas), BLOOD SOCIETY, and A NIGHTMARE ON ELM STREET: THE DREAM DEALERS. Thomas lives in Massachusetts.

Visit the author on Facebook at:
https://www.facebook.com/jeffrey.thomas.71